KATHERINE GARBERA

BABY BUSINESS

Published by Silhouette Books
America's Publisher of Contemporary Romance

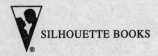

SILHOUETTE BOOKS

ISBN-13: 978-0-373-76888-2
ISBN-10:   0-373-76888-5

BABY BUSINESS

Copyright © 2008 by Katherine Garbera

Printed in U.S.A.

A Baby In The Office!

Donovan carried baby Van in his car seat into the boardroom and set the baby on the table. The women cooed over him while the men stood awkwardly to one side.

"Never saw you as the type who'd bring a kid to work," said Marcus, one of his managers.

Donovan hadn't either. He still wasn't 100 percent certain of himself as a father.

"Let's start the meeting. I'm not sure how long Van will sleep." He moved Van to the side so he was close enough for Donovan to see him but far enough away so that the meeting wouldn't disturb the baby.

"Yes, sir."

He brought the meeting to order, but his mind was only half on business. The other half was on Van... and Cass. He wanted her. As he watched their son sleeping, he realized that his life had changed, whether he was ready to admit it or not.

Dear Reader,

I am enamored with the romantic beauty of Charleston, South Carolina. It's a location steeped in history and tradition and really good food! The perfect setting for a romance, especially if you have one family that is part of the traditional old society and another that is "new money."

My own family embodies both of these things (without the billion dollars!). My dad is descended from the Hathaways, who have been in America since practically the beginning. They have a book, dedicated to them, that traces their lineage. My mother's family are immigrants from Italy who arrived here in 1908. I'm third generation on that side.

In *Baby Business,* Cassidy *should* fit easily into Donovan's world. They both have a lot of money, and family is important to both of them. But Cassidy's family has been in Charleston for only one generation, and although they are wealthy, they don't have the "right" connections. Cassidy and Donovan become a bit like Romeo and Juliet, caught between two families who don't get along.

I wanted to explore how easy it is to fall in love and how hard it is sometimes to make that love work in the real world. I hope you enjoy the outcome.

Happy reading!

Katherine

Recent books by Katherine Garbera

KATHERINE GARBERA

is a strong believer in happily-ever-after. She's written more than thirty-five books and has been nominated for *Romantic Times BOOKreviews* career achievement awards in Series Fantasy and Series Adventure. Her books have appeared on the Waldenbooks bestseller list for series romance and on the *USA TODAY* extended bestseller list. You can visit her on the Web at www.katherinegarbera.com.

This book is dedicated to Courtney and Lucas
for always making me laugh.

One

"**Y**ou're a lifesaver," Cassidy Franzone said as she opened her front door.

At thirty-four weeks pregnant, she needed food when she wanted it. She was single and fine with that. She'd made the choice to have her baby on her own, but she hated going out in Charleston's August heat to pick up her favorite she-crab soup if she didn't have to.

Her father had put his employees at her disposal. If she needed anything, no matter what time of day it was, someone on the staff at Franzone Waste Management was available.

"Am I?"

The man standing in the doorway wasn't her father's employee. In fact, he was the father of her child.

Cassidy gaped at Donovan Tolley. He was still the most attractive man she'd ever seen. His thick hair—hair she'd loved to run her fingers through—lifted in the warm summer breeze. His designer clothes were tailored perfectly to his frame—not for vanity's sake, but because he liked quality.

"What are you doing here?" she asked. She hoped that she sounded nonchalant, as if the reason was not important, but she couldn't help but cover her stomach with one arm protectively. How had Donovan found out that she was pregnant? Or had he?

Maybe it was the fact that she was so hungry, or maybe it had just been so long—almost eight months, to be exact—since she'd seen him. But she felt a sting of tears in the back of her eyes as Donovan smiled at her.

"Can I come in? I don't want to talk to you in the doorway." He seemed a bit dazed. As he pushed his sunglasses up to the top of his head she saw in his eyes that he was busy processing her pregnancy.

"What do you want to talk about?" she asked. What if he didn't believe he was the father of her child? What exactly did he want? And why the hell was she still attracted to this man after he'd broken her heart and left her alone for almost eight months?

He eyed her belly and arched one eyebrow. "Your pregnancy, for starters."

She hadn't told Donovan that she was pregnant with his child, but then again he'd made his views on children quite clear when he'd made his rather businesslike marriage proposal to her. "I know everything I need to about how you feel about kids."

"I'm not so sure about that. Invite me in, Cassidy. I need to talk to you. And I'm not going away."

She hesitated. She would have shut the door on any other man, but then she wouldn't be pregnant with any other man's child. Donovan was the only man she'd ever loved. Still, she didn't need this kind of tension right now.

She was hungry, the baby was moving around and she wasn't exactly sure she wanted to send Donovan on his way. That wasn't like her. She'd always been very decisive, but lately she hadn't been herself.

She felt a bit faint, probably due to the heat. She made up her mind to send Donovan away. She'd deal with him after the baby was born, when she had her act together.

A late-model black-windowed Mercedes pulled into her driveway and Cassidy smiled. Finally her food was here.

"Got your soup, Ms. Cassidy."

"Thank you, Jimmy," she said as the young man

handed her a brown bag. He nodded at her as she took the bag and then he left.

Donovan smiled. "Crab Shack?"

She nodded. She always tried not to focus on the fact that the soup she loved so much came from the place where she and Donovan had eaten at least once a week while they'd been together. The Crab Shack was a famous Charleston institution.

"I'll keep you company while you eat," he said.

"I don't think so. We can talk later this week. I'll call your assistant."

"I'm not leaving, Cassidy."

"Are you going to force your way into my house?" she asked.

"No," he said, bracing one arm on the door frame and leaning in over her. "You're going to invite me in."

His cologne was one-of-a-kind, made for him by an exclusive perfumery in France, and at this moment she really hated that company because Donovan smelled so good. The scent reminded her of the many times she'd lain cuddled close to his side with her head on his chest.

"Cassidy, baby, please let me in," he said, leaning closer so that his words were more of a whisper.

Everything feminine inside of her went nuts. Her breasts felt fuller and her nipples tightened against the fabric of her bra. Her skin felt more sensitive, her lips dry. She wet them with her tongue and saw his eyes narrow as he watched her.

"Is there anything I can do to convince you to go away?"

"No. I've missed you, Cassidy, and leaving is the last thing I want to do."

She hated the little thrill she got when he said he'd missed her. She tried to be nonchalant when she stepped back so that he could enter her house.

Donovan closed the front door behind them and she hesitated in the foyer of her own home. She should have never let him back into her house. She wasn't going to be able to keep any kind of distance between them. Face-to-face with Donovan again, all she could think about was sex. About being back in his arms one last time. Her hormones had been going crazy throughout her pregnancy, and once again they came rushing to the fore. She wanted this man. She hadn't even tried dating in the last eight months, though a few brave guys had asked her out. She didn't want anyone but Donovan.

She led the way to the first floor screened-in porch. It overlooked the wooded area behind her house, and with its tall ceilings and the shade provided by the nearby oak and magnolia trees, it was a cool refuge from the heat.

"Can I get you a beer or tea?" she asked.

"Beer would be great," he said.

She set her soup on the table and went to the wet bar to get Donovan's beer. He liked Heineken, same as she did. Though she hadn't had a beer since she'd gotten pregnant, she still kept her refrigerator stocked for when her brothers and friends visited.

She grabbed a bottle of Pellegrino for herself and came back to the table. Donovan stood up and held her chair for her. The gentlemanly courtesy was one he had always performed, and she appreciated it. That was one of the things that had always set Donovan apart from other men. She thanked him and sat down.

Food suddenly became unimportant as she realized the man she loved was sitting there next to her. She had to clasp her hands in her lap to keep from reaching out to touch him. To keep from leaning across the table and making sure he was really there.

"How are you, Cassidy?" he asked.

"Good. I haven't had any complications from the pregnancy." She was twenty-eight years old and in great shape thanks to a lifetime of exercise and eating right. The baby was healthy, something that she sometimes fancied was due to the fact that she and Donovan had been so much in love when he'd been conceived. But she knew that was her imagination running away with her.

"I'm glad."

"Are you?" she asked, trying for sarcasm but guessing she'd sounded a bit pleased that he was concerned about her health.

"Yes." He leaned back in his chair. "Why didn't you tell me about the baby? I'm assuming the baby is mine."

She suspected he knew she wasn't interested in any other man. She hadn't hidden her feelings for him when they were together.

"Yes, it is yours. I didn't tell you because it didn't seem like the type of information you'd be interested in."

"What do you mean by that?"

"Just that if something doesn't involve Tolley-Patterson Manufacturing or any of your other business interests, you usually don't pay much attention to it."

"I paid attention to you," he said.

"When there wasn't a crisis at one of your companies, sure, you did pay attention to me."

But she had always been aware that his position as executive vice president at Tolley-Patterson, the company his family owned, was the most important thing in Donovan's life. He was also consumed by his other business interests, and with increasing his holdings. He co-owned a sporting goods company with his former college roommate, and he had an interest in an island resort on Tobago with a friend from his boarding-school days. For a while his constant focus on business hadn't mattered. But during the last few months, while they'd been apart, she'd come to realize she had sold herself short in their relationship.

Donovan had always been obsessed with proving there was more to him than just his trust fund. And she wasn't interested in competing for his attention again. Getting over Donovan had been hard. The hardest thing she'd ever gone through. She'd thought she wasn't going to recover at first, and when she'd gotten confirmation that she was pregnant with his child, she'd made up her mind that the baby was the reason she'd been brought into Donovan's life. His child would be the one on whom she'd pour all the love that he'd never really wanted from her.

But now he was back, and she had this tingly excitement in the pit of her stomach that made her hope he might be back for good.

And that scared her more than facing the future alone.

"What does that comment mean? I never ignored you when we were together."

Donovan was still trying to process the fact that Cassidy was having his baby. He couldn't believe his good fortune in finding her pregnant. He'd come here today to ask her to marry him again, to convince her that he'd changed his mind about family. And he had to do it without revealing the circumstances that had brought him to her doorstep today.

Donovan had forgotten how truly beautiful Cassidy was. Her skin was like porcelain, fine and pale, and her hair was rich and thick. He knew from experience how soft it felt against his skin. Her lips were full, and though she didn't have lipstick on, they were a perfect deep pink color—the exact same shade as her nipples. God, he wanted to forget about talking and just draw her into his arms and kiss her. How he'd missed her mouth….

His body hardened and he adjusted his legs, trying to quell his erection. He'd never thought of pregnant women as sensual before, but there was something about seeing Cassidy's lush body filled out with his child.

"Only because I knew that you needed to be at work twelve hours a day and on weekends…I didn't make a lot of demands on your time," she said.

It took a moment for her words to register, because he'd been watching her mouth and wondering…if he leaned over and kissed her, would she kiss him back?

But then the words registered and he realized that she probably wasn't in the mood to be kissed. She was busy focusing on all the reasons they were no longer together. And he needed to get her thinking about why they should be again.

If there was one thing that Donovan was good at, it was winning—and winning Cassidy over was his first priority. He was competitive, and his drive for success went much deeper than wanting to make money. God knew, with his trust fund he never needed to work a day in his life. And the investments he'd made in the ventures with his friends had paid off handsomely. But he wanted more. He wanted his birthright—the CEO position at Tolley-Patterson.

Looking at Cassidy with her beautiful hair curling around her face made him realize that he'd missed her far more than he'd realized. He wouldn't have come back on his own, without the incentive of needing a wife and child, but being here now, he knew that coming back was exactly what he'd needed to do. Her pregnancy simply made his objective that much easier to attain.

"I'm sorry," he said. And part of him really meant the words. Another part—the man who was always looking for a way to turn every situation to his advantage—knew that being humble would help him win Cassidy back. Knew that even though he'd hurt her, there was a tentative hope in her eyes.

"For?"

"Making you feel like you weren't first in my life," he said.

She fiddled with her food bag and drew out a foam container of what he suspected was she-crab soup.

"Don't play games with me, Donovan."

"I'm not."

"Yes, you are. You're a master game player and everything you do is for a specific purpose."

She knew him well. In fact, that was one reason he'd let the distance grow between them when she'd walked out on him. She knew him better than he wanted anyone to know him. But she was the key to what he needed, and he wasn't going to let her walk away again. This time, he was better able to make room for Cassidy in his life.

"What? No snappy comeback?" she asked.

"Sarcasm doesn't suit you."

She shrugged. "I'm pregnant. Most of the time that means I get a pass on things like that."

"Does it?"

"Yes."

"From who?"

"Everyone." She gave him a grin that was pure Cassidy for sexiness. She had a way of accepting her feminine appeal and knew its effect on everyone she met.

"Is there a man in your life?" he asked, abruptly realizing that she might have met someone after they'd broken up. Oh, he knew the baby was his. Not just because she'd confirmed it, but because he knew Cassidy. She'd said she loved him, and he knew that, to her, that meant more than just words.

"My dad and brothers," she said, looking down at the table, the joy she'd exhibited a moment earlier totally extinguished.

"I meant a boyfriend," he said.

"Yeah, right. I'm pregnant out to here with your baby, why the heck would I be dating someone else?" she said, looking up at him with those clear brown eyes of hers.

"How long are we going to be dealing with the sarcasm? I didn't know you were pregnant," he said.

"I didn't think you'd care."

"Well, I do. So you're not dating?" he asked one more time. He couldn't help the rush of satisfaction that swamped him when he realized she'd been alone for the months they'd been apart.

"No. It didn't seem fair to get involved with another man right now. What about you, are you dating anyone?"

"Would I be here if I was?" he asked. The truth was he'd buried himself even more in work after they'd parted. That was one reason he'd had an edge over his cousin Sam, his competition for the CEO position. Sam had been married for more than ten years now and divided his time between the office and home. Then their grandfather's will had evened things up between them.

"Why are you here?" Cassidy asked.

He scratched the back of his neck. He knew what

to say, but as he looked at her he began to calculate the consequences of what he was about to do. Lying to Cassidy wasn't something he did lightly. But if he told her the truth—that thanks to his grandfather's will, to take over as CEO of Tolley-Patterson, he needed to be married and have a child within a year as well as win the vote of the board—she'd tell him to hit the road.

"Donovan?"

"I missed you, Cassidy."

"I've been right here," she said.

"I wasn't sure you'd take me back."

"You want to date again?" she asked. "Once the baby is born that will be difficult."

"I don't want to date you, I want to marry you. The last eight months have made me realize how much I want you as my wife. I came here today prepared to tell you I've changed my mind about having a family."

He heard her breath catch in her throat and saw a sheen of tears in her eyes.

He pushed back from the table, standing up and walking over to her chair. He pulled it away from the table and turned her to face him. She looked up at him.

He leaned down so that their lips were almost touching. Framing her face with his hands, he suddenly knew that he really didn't want to screw this up. And not just because he wanted to beat Sam. He wanted to do this right because Cassidy was the key to a life that he'd never realized he might want until this moment.

"I want to marry you, Cassidy Franzone. I want to be a father to our child and have that family you dreamed we'd have together."

With Donovan so close to her, all Cassidy really wanted to do was kiss him and wrap her arms around him, feel his arms around her and maybe rest her head against his chest for a while. It was what she woke up in the middle of the night longing for, that touch of his.

But Donovan had been so adamant that he wasn't going to have a family, and this change, though eight months in the making, was drastic for him.

"Why? What made you change your mind?"

"I missed you," he said.

But he'd said that before. And missing her wasn't an explanation of why he'd changed his feelings about kids.

"That's not why you suddenly want a family." She was afraid to trust the sudden turnaround in his attitude.

He moved and dropped his hands from her face as he stood up. He grabbed his beer from the table and paced to the railing of the porch. Leaning one hip on the wooden railing, he tipped his head back and drained the bottle.

"What do you want me to say, Cassidy?"

She had no idea. Eight months ago when he'd proposed to her, she'd suspected she was pregnant—and she'd walked away when he'd made his opinion on kids and family clear. She'd walked away, because she knew that Donovan was the type of man who'd marry a woman he'd gotten pregnant—and that wasn't why she wanted to be married. She needed Donovan to marry her because he was in love with her. Because he couldn't live without her the way she couldn't live without him.

"I want to know why you changed your mind. You said kids were the major source of all arguments between married couples. You said that having a child ruined many of the great relationships you'd seen. You said—"

"Hell, I know what I said."

"And?"

"I've had a lot of time to think about you and me, Cassidy. The way we were with each other, the way we were both raised… I think we can have a family and not lose the essence of who we are as a couple."

He was saying things that she wanted to believe, things that she'd dreamed of him saying, and a part of her wanted to just say yes. But being alone had made her realize that being in love wasn't the be-all and end-all of a relationship. And she couldn't go through getting over him again.

"Are you proposing because you found out I'm pregnant? I don't want you to marry me because you feel obligated."

Donovan crossed the porch back to her. He set his beer bottle on the table and drew her to her feet. "Cassidy, I wouldn't insult either of us that way. I'm here because I need you. I was coming to see you today to beg you to take me back."

"Does it have anything to do with your grandfather's death?" she asked. "I was sorry to hear of his passing." She'd sent flowers and felt awful for not going to the service.

Donovan couldn't believe how close to the truth she'd come with that one innocent comment. "Losing Granddaddy did make me realize how quickly life can change, and I thought about how much he'd always wanted me to have children of my own while he could see them. I thought we had more time…"

Cassidy wrapped an arm around his shoulder and hugged him briefly then stepped back. "Did that make you realize there was more to life than work?"

Cassidy knew how hard it was for Donovan to talk about his emotions. But if she was going to take a chance on him again, on letting herself really love him and bring up a child with him, then she needed to know where he stood.

It wasn't just about her anymore. She rubbed a

hand over her stomach, thinking of her baby—their baby. She wanted the best for this child, and that meant two loving parents.

"I guess it did. I don't want to talk too much about it. Granddaddy and I butted heads a lot, and his heart attack was so sudden…."

Donovan and Maxwell Patterson had had what could kindly be called an adversarial relationship. "Did you get a chance to make peace with him?"

"No, not really. Our last words were spoken in anger. I walked out on him."

"I'm sure he knew you loved him."

Donovan shrugged as though it wasn't important but she knew that he'd always had a driving need to make his grandfather proud of him. To prove to the family that he was more than his sculptor father's son. To prove that he had the same blood in his veins as his grandfather did.

"That's why I need you. I need to have you by my side. You and our child. I don't want to get to the end of my days and find I have nothing but Tolley-Patterson to show for it. I want you to marry me, Cassidy."

Her heart melted. She still thought there had to be more to his change of heart, but she didn't care. He was offering her more than she'd ever expected him to. Donovan was the kind of man who honored his commitments. And with their baby on the way she knew that she could make their life everything she always dreamed it would be.

"Um…"

"What?"

"Getting married now, like this," she said, gesturing to her stomach, "isn't what I had in mind. I want to have a big wedding and all that."

"What are you saying?"

"Um…" What *was* she saying? She wanted their child to be born with Donovan's name. But a public wedding was out of the question until she delivered their child. "I think I'm saying let's get married in secret, with just our families present, and then after the baby is here we can have a big public commitment ceremony."

Donovan hadn't thought beyond getting Cassidy to agree to marry him. Married in secret didn't seem like a plan that would fulfill the conditions of his grandfather's will. His lawyer was working on finding a loophole, but Granddaddy had been a smart man—he'd made sure that his bizarre requirements for the next CEO of Tolley-Patterson were legally sound. It didn't matter that everyone who'd heard the will and read the new CEO description thought it was crazy. Legally Granddaddy had followed every rule.

"Why do you want to keep the marriage secret?"

Cassidy flushed and wrapped her arms around

her stomach. One hand rubbed the top of her baby bump. "I just don't want the world to think that you're marrying me for the child."

"Cassidy, that's silly. Who cares what the world thinks?"

"I do," she said quietly.

"Then, okay, we'll do it your way."

"Really?"

"Yes."

"Thank you."

"You're welcome," he said, drawing her into his arms. The exhalation of her breath on a sigh brushed against his neck as she wrapped her arms around his waist and melted against him. Because of her belly, the embrace was different from all the ones they'd shared in the past, but Donovan felt a new sense of rightness to having her in his arms.

No matter why he was back here with her, this was where he was meant to be. She tipped her head back and he looked down into her brown eyes.

He cupped her face in his hands and lowered his mouth to hers. She rose on tiptoe to meet him. He brushed his lips over hers once, twice, and then he felt her lips part and her tongue touch his lower lip.

He'd never forgotten Cassidy's kisses. She was the only woman he'd ever found who fit him perfectly physically. There had never been any awkwardness to their sex life. She tasted wonderful to him, and as he slipped his tongue into her mouth he realized just how much he'd missed the taste of her.

She held on to him as she tilted her head to give him deeper access to her mouth. He tunneled his fingers into her hair, caressing the sides of her neck with his thumbs. She moaned deep in her throat, and the sound made him groan and slide one hand down to her hips to draw her closer to him.

She shifted against him, and then he felt a nudge against his stomach. It knocked him off track. He pulled back and looked down at her belly. A bump moved under her maternity top.

"Uh…"

She smiled. "He gets active in the afternoon."

"He?"

"Yes. We're having a son."

"A son," he said. Thinking about the baby as the means to an end was different than this. My God, he was going to have a son. That rocked him more than finding Cassidy pregnant. He sat down in the chair that Cassidy had vacated. She stood there watching him.

"Are you okay?"

"Yes. I just didn't think about the baby beyond you being pregnant. You know?"

She smiled at him. "Yes, I do. It's one thing to be pregnant but another to picture the baby in the future, isn't it?"

"Yes, it is. So I want to do this as soon as possible."

"Do this? You mean get married?" she asked.

"Yes. I'll take care of getting all the paperwork in order."

"Okay. I want to have our ceremony at my parents' house on the beach."

"That's fine. You can make the arrangements. When is the baby due?"

"In less than two weeks."

"Then I think we should get married over the weekend."

"So soon?"

"We don't have a lot of time if we're going to be married when our son is born."

"Does that matter to you?"

"Yes," he said, realizing that it did matter. He wanted to do everything by the book so that when the lawyers looked at his marriage to Cassidy and the birth of their son, they'd have no questions. And he needed to be married to her before she had his child. His primitive instincts demanded that she have his name.

"I'll give my mom a call and see if they can host the ceremony this weekend. Adam is in New York, so I'll have to see if he can make it back."

"Will both of your brothers be there?" he asked, guessing that the Franzone boys weren't too happy with him.

"I hope so. Don't worry, they understood about me having the baby on my own."

Somehow Donovan doubted that. Her two brothers were older and superprotective. He'd done his best to avoid them since he and Cassidy had broken up.

The late-afternoon sun spilled onto the porch, lighting the deep dark sheen of her hair and making him catch his breath. She was truly the most beautiful woman in the world. And he couldn't believe how easily this had all gone.

But then, this was Cassidy, and she'd always made his life brighter just by being near him. He would never admit it out loud, but maybe Granddaddy had done him a favor when he'd added that clause to the CEO requirements.

As he listened to her speaking with her mother, he realized that she was hopeful about their marriage. He made a vow at that moment to never let her find out why he'd come back. He'd do whatever it took to protect Cassidy from learning that he'd returned to her only to win the CEO position at Tolley-Patterson.

Two

Dwelling on details wasn't something that Cassidy was good at, and she knew it was one of the areas where Donovan and she weren't the same. He kept talking about all of the things that had to be done, but it was the first week in August and she was bigger than a beached whale—and about as comfortable as one, as well.

"Are you listening to me?" Donovan asked.

He'd coaxed her out of her house and to the country club where both of their families were members. They were sitting in a secluded alcove overlooking the ocean and she could feel the warm breeze stirring over the veranda.

"No."

"Cassidy, we don't have much time and I want everything taken care of before you go into labor."

"I don't understand what the rush is," she said, a part of her not believing that Donovan was back in her life. But here he was, and he was taking over the way he had before.

And she wasn't too sure she wanted to let him. The last time, she'd been more than happy for him to take the lead, but she was older and wiser—and crankier, she thought. She didn't want to talk about what kind of life insurance policy they should have for themselves to protect the baby if they died.

She didn't want to think about anything like that.

"We need to talk about guardians, as well. I think it would be best if the child went with my family."

"What do you mean, best? I've already asked Adam to be the guardian." Her oldest brother was very responsible and she knew that Adam would keep her child safe.

"You shouldn't have done that without consulting me first."

"Um…you weren't in my life, remember?"

"Again with the sarcasm."

"Yeah, I kind of like it."

"I don't."

"Then stop trying to run my life. I said I'd marry

you, but I'm not going to let you take complete control of everything."

"Cassidy…"

"Yes?"

"I'm not asking you to let me control your life."

"You're not?"

He leaned across the table. There was a glint in his eyes that was distinctly sexual and she had to fight not to smile. This was the Donovan she remembered, able to turn any situation into something fun and sexy.

"No, I'm not…I'm telling you."

She leaned closer to him. Her belly rested against the lip of the wooden surface. She reached out and traced his lower lip, and his mouth opened. She shifted farther in her chair and briefly pressed her lips to his. "You have to remember one thing, Donovan Tolley."

"And that is?" He brushed his mouth against hers. The soft kiss might have looked sweet and innocent, but a flood of hormones rushed through her body. Even though she was very pregnant, she really wanted this man.

"You aren't the boss outside of Tolley-Patterson."

He stroked a finger down the side of her neck, tracing the bead of sweat that had just taken the same path. "Once we're married I will be."

"How do you figure?" she asked, trying to ignore the way his finger felt as he stroked her skin just above the base of her neck. Her pulse was beating wildly. She had no idea where this conversation was going; she only knew that this was what she had missed. Having Donovan in her life meant she wasn't alone. And she could just be herself, no matter how crazy or silly she might seem to someone else.

"I'm going to insist that our vows have the word *obey* in them."

"I have no problem with that," she said. "I've always wanted you to obey me."

He threw his head back and laughed, drawing the attention of the other people on the veranda. Cassidy smiled at him and leaned back in her seat, taking a sip of the refreshingly cool lemonade she'd ordered.

Donovan's BlackBerry twittered and he pulled it from his pocket, glanced at the screen and then up at her. "I have to make a quick call. Will you be okay by yourself?"

She nodded. He got up and left the table, and she glanced around. Sitting alone at a table in a restaurant always made her feel exposed, something that she didn't like. She took a sip of her water.

"Cassidy?"

She turned to see her best friend, Emma Graham, and Emma's fiancé, Paul Preston. "Emma! How are you?"

"Good. Are you here alone?"

"No. I'm with Donovan."

Emma raised both eyebrows and told Paul she'd

meet him at their table. Emma wasn't a subtle person, and Cassidy immediately knew her best friend was concerned.

"What's going on?" Emma asked, sitting down in Donovan's seat. "The man left you alone and pregnant. I can't believe he'd have the gall to come back to you now."

"You know he didn't know I was pregnant."

"Okay, I'll give him that. What does he want?"

"To marry me."

Emma's eyes widened. "Are you going to?" she asked.

For the first time, Cassidy felt a twinge about how easily she'd capitulated. But she couldn't have done anything else. Surely Emma understood—she was getting married as well. Cassidy wanted a partner— a husband—in her life. "Yes. I think so. I mean…"

"You still think you love him."

"Who's to say that I don't love him?"

Emma shrugged one delicate shoulder. "No one but you. Are we happy about this?"

Cassidy thought about it. "I don't know yet. I was going to call you in the morning."

"I've got an early flight to New York for a meeting. I can talk until eight tonight and then again after three tomorrow. I was going to stop by your place later today anyway."

They had grown up together and attended the

same boarding school in Connecticut. Emma was like the sister Cassidy had never had and had always wanted. "Did you tell him about the baby, is that why he came back?"

"No. He just showed up."

"Why?"

"Um, he missed me," she said to her friend, feeling sheepish and suddenly wondering what Emma would say.

"And you believe that?" Emma asked.

"I—"

"Yes, Emma, she does believe me, because I told her that letting her walk out of my life was the biggest mistake I'd ever made."

"It's about time you realized it," Emma said. "Hurt her again and you'll deal with me."

Donovan nodded as Emma gave Cassidy a hug and then walked away. The threat should have seemed silly coming from the petite brunette, but Donovan knew Emma Graham was more than capable of backing up her words.

"Sorry about that," Cassidy said as he sat back down.

"It's okay. She cares for you and wants the best for you."

"Yes, she does."

Cassidy took a sip of her lemonade and glanced

toward the ocean. Donovan realized that getting her agreement to the marriage wasn't enough. He needed to…ah, hell, he needed to make some promises that would alleviate Cassidy's fears that he was going to hurt her again.

"I care, too," he said, realizing as the words left his mouth how lame they sounded. Lame-ass comments like that were exactly why he didn't talk about his emotions. He was much better keeping things light or talking about business.

"I'd suspected as much, since you asked me to marry you."

"See, you are a smart girl."

"Don't be condescending."

"I wasn't. You're one of the smartest women I know. It's what drew me to you the first time."

"Um…I thought that was my legs."

It had been everything about her. Her long legs in that impossibly short micromini she'd had on. Her long, dark curly hair hanging down her back in silky waves. But, to tell the truth, it had been her laughter that had first caught his attention. It was deep and un-inhibited. He'd found himself distracted at the charity event. Instead of conducting business as he usually did at social functions, he'd followed her and joined her group just to hear that laugh again. And her intelligence was quickly evident as she debated and discussed myriad current events.

"Your legs were part of it," he said. He'd always been a leg man.

"I was drawn to your eyes."

"My eyes?" he asked, wondering what she saw in them.

"Every time you looked at me, there was this intensity that made me feel like I was the only person in the room that night."

"You were the only one I saw," he admitted.

"Yeah, until Sam entered and you remembered that he's your rival."

"That's not completely true." But it was partially true. He and Sam had always been in competition with each other. They'd been born a week apart and Donovan was the younger of the two of them. Every summer they'd been sent to live with their grandfather, and the old man had always challenged the both of them. Donovan had learned early on that the key to Granddaddy's praise was winning.

"Yes, it is. You even told me you'd do anything to beat him to the vice presidency, and you did it."

"That's right. You said you liked my ambition," he said.

"Did I?"

He nodded, wishing he knew what she was thinking at this moment. Because he had a feeling she was recalling the other things about him, the things she didn't like. Or had merely tolerated.

Part of the reason he'd let things lie between them was that she made him vulnerable, and only a man without any weaknesses could fully protect himself. Because then he had nothing for his enemies to attack.

He knew that sounded melodramatic considering he was an executive, but the modern-day business world was just as fierce as the ancient fiefdoms that had been defended by nobles and warriors. And Donovan had always known he was a warrior. The need to win was strongly bred into him.

"I like you when you're happy, and competing does that for you."

"You do that for me, too."

She tipped her head to the side. "Really?"

"Mmm, hmm. Want to get out of here and go for a walk on the beach?"

"No. Sorry, but my feet are swollen. I know that sounds totally unromantic, but I'm not up to a long walk on the beach until it's cooler."

"How about going out on the yacht? You can sit on the deck and feel the ocean breeze in your hair."

She hesitated.

"What?"

"I can't believe that you're back in my life and going on about everything as if nothing has changed. As if the last eight months never happened…but they did, and I…I'm not sure if I can trust you the way I did before."

Donovan rubbed his neck and looked away. What could he say to her? He needed Cassidy and their child. And he needed them now. He didn't have time to seduce her or convince her that he was the man she wanted in her life.

He put his sunglasses on and stood up. "I can't just stand around and pretend we have all the time in the world to reconnect."

"Because of the baby?" she asked.

There was something in her tone and a kind of worry in her eyes that told him he had to say the right thing at this moment. Dammit, he sucked at saying the right thing.

"Not just because of the baby, Cassidy. Because you and I have lost eight months and we have only a short time to find *us* again before we are going to have our child."

Tears glimmered in her eyes and he shook his head. "You know I stink at saying the right thing."

She held his gaze. "Sometimes you say exactly the right thing."

"Don't bet on it happening too often."

She chuckled and gave him a weak grin. She looked tired and so achingly beautiful that he wanted to just pull her into his arms and hold her forever. Never mind the warning flashing at the back of his mind that he had a meeting with the board of directors to prepare for.

"Come out on the yacht, just for an hour," he said.

* * *

Cassidy loved being out on the ocean. The wind was cooler out here. Donovan had seated her on the padded bench and gone to make arrangements with the captain of the yacht. He hadn't come back since they'd left the dock.

She didn't mind, though; it gave her time to regroup. She put one hand low on her belly and felt the baby's foot resting against the outer wall of her stomach. She was overwhelmed by Donovan and everything that he was doing right now. A part of her knew that this was his way of ensuring she married him. That he would do whatever he had to in this week leading up to the wedding. That was the way he'd been when they'd first started dating. He was really good at making her feel like his top priority when he wanted to.

Had she trusted him too much?

Her cell phone rang and she glanced at the caller ID. Adam. She didn't answer it. She wasn't up to a lecture from her oldest brother at this moment, and that was exactly what she'd get from him. She guessed that their mother had put the word out to the family that she and Donovan were back together and getting married next weekend.

She had a feeling that her brothers weren't going to be very welcoming to Donovan.

Her phone beeped to let her know she had a voice mail. She would listen to it later.

"Who was that?"

"Adam."

"You didn't answer it?"

"I'm not really up to another demanding male telling me what he thinks is best for me."

"Demanding male? Is that how you see me?" Donovan asked.

"Yes. You've been bullying me all afternoon."

"It's because I do know best," he said, handing her a glass of sparkling water with a twist of lime.

She took a sip and watched him through narrowed eyes. She was glad that the sun was still drifting in the sky, because it gave her an excuse to keep her sunglasses on.

"You don't know me these days," she said. "How can you know what's best?"

"I do know you, Cassidy. I know that you are loving and caring. And that you've always wanted a family, and that despite having a career you love, work has never come first for you."

That was very true. Her job as curator at a small museum in Charleston was nice, but it wasn't anything that could compare with being a mom. She was going to stay on at her position in a part-time capacity once her son was born.

She had never tried to pretend that family and relationships weren't important to her. Her father and Adam were so consumed with their jobs that she'd been soured on that kind of career when she was a young girl. There had to be more to life than work, in her opinion.

"But you don't feel that way, do you? Or is that something else that's changed since we've been apart?"

"No. I haven't changed my focus. But I have broadened it to include more than just Tolley-Patterson."

"Like what? I know about your other business interests."

"Of course I still have those. I've also invested in Gil's team for the America's Cup. He has a new design that's going to revolutionize yacht racing."

"That's still an investment. How have you changed to put relationships and people first?"

"Gil is one of my oldest friends."

"I've never met him," she said. She had noticed that most of Donovan's friends didn't contact him unless they needed money. To be fair, he didn't exactly encourage anyone to stay close to him. He was a bit of a loner, despite his social connections and the parties he frequented. She'd realized early on that he was pretty much all about business.

"We'll invite him to our public wedding," he said.

"Fine, but you still haven't convinced me that you know what's best for *me*."

"I don't have to convince you with words," he said. "I'm going to show you with actions."

She raised her eyebrows. "How?"

He rubbed a hand through his hair. "You'll have to wait and see."

"I will?"

"Yes." He paused, and she braced herself, guessing she wouldn't like what was coming next. "I called my parents and they're both home this evening. When we get back to shore I think we should drop by and tell them about the wedding."

Cassidy tried to keep her face expressionless.

"It won't be bad."

"Your mom doesn't like me. She thinks my family are white trash."

"That's not true. She asked about you after we broke up."

"Really?"

"Yes. And we can't be married without my parents there. They would be disappointed."

Cassidy doubted that. But family was important and Donovan's parents would be her baby's grandparents. Maybe knowing that she was pregnant with Donovan's baby would make Donovan's mother like her better.

Not that being liked was *too* important to Cassidy, but she hated the fact that Donovan's family always acted so superior simply because they'd been in Charleston forever.

She gritted her teeth and mentally prepared herself to face Donovan's mother.

Three

Donovan's family had lived in the same house for more than six generations. The 1858 mansion was registered as a historical landmark. The first Tolley family had moved to Charleston just after the Civil War. They traced their fortune back to those days, as well.

His mother was a member of the Junior League and the Charleston Preservation Society, and she sat on the board for directors of Tolley-Patterson. She prided herself on the work she did with that group. She was the kind of woman who never had a hair out of place, and family image was very important to her.

"You're getting *married?*" she asked as she and

Donovan sat in the parlor. She had a martini in one hand and looked every inch the genteel Southern lady that she was.

Cassidy was outside walking through the lamplit gardens with his father. His parents had both been shocked to see a pregnant Cassidy, and had covered their reaction only so-so. Donovan had been grateful when his usually withdrawn father had jumped up and asked to show his soon-to-be daughter-in-law his latest sculpture.

"Yes."

"I thought you broke up."

"We did, but now we're back together and getting married."

"Is this because of your grandfather's will? Even though she's pregnant, it might not be your child. Donovan, darling, there are a lot of women more suited to your social station that you could marry."

"Cassidy *is* suited to our station, Mother. And she's the one I chose."

"What about the baby?"

"Mother."

"Yes?"

"Stop it. I need you to just be happy for me and go along with this."

"I'll try, dear. It's just…I'm a little young to be a grandmother."

"And everyone will say that, you know that."

"Do you know if it's a boy or a girl?"

"A boy."

His mother took another sip of her martini. He couldn't read her thoughts. But she did smile for a second.

"Will her family be at the wedding? Surely you aren't going to have a big wedding with the pregnancy so far along."

"No, Mrs. Tolley, we aren't going to have a big wedding. Just an intimate ceremony at my parents' house. And we hope you'll both be there."

Donovan glanced at Cassidy to gauge her mood, but her face looked serene. She smiled politely at his mom. He had never thought before about the kind of attitude that Cassidy must have to endure from the oldest established families in Charleston. Her family, though wealthier than many, had accrued their fortune in the last twenty years and didn't have the kind of pedigree that the women in the Junior League approved of.

"I heard your parents were doing some remodeling," his mother said. "Would you consider having the ceremony here?"

Cassidy glanced at him and he shrugged. Everyone had heard about the bright pink stucco that been used to repaint the Franzone mansion. Two weeks worth of editorials on the eyesore that their mansion had become had ensured that.

The Franzones were in the middle of a lengthy

battle with their contractor to get him to repaint the house. The color was so bright and gaudy that the neighbors had complained to city hall in hopes of forcing the Franzones to do something immediately, instead of waiting for legal settlement.

"Thank you for that kind offer, but my mom has already started making arrangements."

"Very well. When is the ceremony going to be?"

Donovan knew from his mother's tone that she wasn't happy, but he didn't care. He needed Cassidy to be his wife. And his mother was never going to be happy to be related by marriage to the Franzones.

"This Saturday, Mother," Donovan said. He walked to Cassidy's side and wrapped his arm around her, pulling her close to him.

"Where is your father?"

"He went back to his studio," Cassidy answered. "He showed me the sculpture he's working on for the Myerson Museum."

"Did he?" Donovan and his father hardly had what anyone would call a close relationship, but he'd hoped that today, since he had come over to an-nounce his engagement, his father would leave his studio for more than an hour and spend some time with him. But that wasn't the type of man his father was, and Donovan was old enough to accept that.

His parents had never had a close relationship. They'd married because his grandfather had wanted to merge Tolley Industries and Patterson Manufacturing. He'd always been aware that his parents didn't have a love match. His father's M.O. was to retreat to his studio whenever possible.

"Yes, he did. It's still rough, but you can see that it'll be breathtaking when it's done."

"I'm sure it will," Donovan said. "Mother, would you like to join us for dinner?"

"No, thank you, Donovan. I have a bridge game tonight."

"We will see you Saturday, then? At the Franzones'?" he asked.

"Of course. What time on Saturday?" she asked.

"Cassidy?"

She pulled her BlackBerry phone out and pressed a few buttons. "Six-thirty, Mrs. Tolley. There will be a dinner afterward."

"Do you need me to do anything to help?"

"No, thank you. We've got it all taken care of."

They said their goodbyes and were outside a few minutes later. Cassidy let out a breath.

"What?"

"Nothing."

"Cassidy, I know something's on your mind."

"Do I really need to tell you how snobby your mother is? She'll probably have a fit when she realizes that I've asked Emma to be one of the witnesses for the ceremony."

"Emma's not family."

"I don't have any sisters, and you know she's like one to me." She smiled shyly. "Do you want me to ask one of my brothers to be the best man?"

He stared at her. He hadn't thought about who should be his witness. "Which one?"

"Adam makes the most sense. You've met him."

He and Adam Franzone didn't get along. From the very beginning of his relationship with Cassidy, Adam had been telling him he wasn't good enough for her.

He didn't want her brother to stand up with him, but if it meant keeping Cassidy happy, he guessed he could do it. He shrugged. "Adam will do."

Donovan was silent as they drove away from his parents' house. Cassidy wondered if she was making the biggest mistake of her life. She'd been seeing Donovan as she wanted him to be. Seeing him with his mother, so arrogant and very much the wealthy son who'd always gotten his way…

"What are you thinking?" he asked.

"Nothing," she said. There were some doubts that she couldn't shake. She was waiting for the other shoe to drop, and that was exactly why she couldn't shake the panicked feeling deep inside of her.

"So it's something you don't want to share with me," he said, his voice a deep rumble in the cockpit of his sports car.

"How do you know I'm thinking anything at all?" Cassidy asked.

"Baby, you always have something going on in your head. Is it about work?"

"No. Lately I've been working with an artist, Sandra Paulo, who isn't coming in until a month after the baby is born. And she's been very cooperative. She shipped all of her paintings early so I'd be able to plan the display before I go out on maternity leave."

"Well if it's not the job, is it family?"

"Whose?"

"Mine or yours," he said.

"Not really. I mean, your mom *is* a bit of snob—that tone in her voice when she talked about the ceremony being held at my parents' place was a bit obvious."

"She's just used to things being a certain way."

"I imagine she is. You know your family is too caught up in pedigree."

Donovan shrugged. "So that's what you were thinking about? I can't change my mother's attitude."

"I know, it's a part of who she is. It really doesn't bother me at all. I only mentioned it because you brought the subject up."

"I didn't bring it up. I asked what was on your mind, and you still haven't told me."

"That's because it's a nice day and I don't want to start an argument."

Donovan glanced over at her and arched one eyebrow at her. "I won't argue with you, Cassidy."

"I know that. You get quiet and clam up and act like nothing is wrong."

"I sound like a sulky two-year-old."

She forced herself not to smile. "Well...if the shoe fits."

He reached over and tickled her thigh, making her squirm in her seat. Laughing put too much pressure on her bladder.

"Stop, Donovan."

"Not until you take that back."

"Okay, I take it back," she said. He stopped tickling her, caressing the inside of her thigh before he removed his hand.

"You're so incredibly sexy," he said, his voice deepening with lust.

"I'm not sexy at all. I'm almost nine months pregnant. Big as a whale."

He pulled off the road under a streetlamp. "Cassidy, look at me."

She faced him. She'd never really had body issues, but the bigger her stomach had gotten and the skinnier her friends had stayed, the more conscious she'd become of her size. Being alone all these months hadn't helped, either.

He leaned over her and released her seat belt and

then his own. He drew her into his arms and held her close.

"You are the only woman in the world who is always beautiful to me. First thing in the morning, after a workout, sunburned and swollen." He tipped her head back and leaned in to kiss her. "You've always been beautiful to me, but never more so than now. You are carrying my child."

He pulled back and put his hand on her belly. "I thought my life was meant to follow one path. Business has always been my focus. But when our baby kicked against me the other night...it was like an awakening for me."

"Awakening how?" she asked. This was what she wanted to understand. This was what she needed to know. Was Donovan really back because he'd had a change of heart and needed her the way she needed him? This moment could change everything. Put her doubts to rest for good.

"It made me realize that our futures—my future and yours—were intertwined. And it made me see that I had a chance to leave behind a legacy outside of Tolley-Patterson."

Cassidy started to ask another question, but he stopped her with his mouth. The kiss was soft but not tentative. It felt like a promise to her. The promise of a life that they would build together with their child.

He sucked her bottom lip between his teeth and

nibbled on her. She shifted in his arms, trying to get closer to him, but the close confines of the car made it impossible.

He groaned, his hands skimming up her belly to brush over her breasts. They were sensitive and his touch on them made her squirm as a pulse of desire speared through her body.

"Donovan," she said, holding tight to his shoulders when he would have pulled back.

"Baby," he said. "God, I want you."

"I want you, too," she said, thinking of all the vivid sexual dreams she'd had of him during her pregnancy.

He kissed her again and this time there was nothing soft or tentative about it. He was reclaiming her, and she knew that if they weren't in the front seat of his sports car this encounter wouldn't end until he was buried deep inside her body. But instead he gentled the embrace with some light kisses and eventually put her back in her seat, fastening her seat belt.

"Don't worry about us, Cassidy. We are solid this time. I'm not going to let you go."

As he pulled back out into traffic, she smiled, believing in Donovan and the future they'd have together.

Donovan dropped off Cassidy at her place and turned to leave. He had a meeting with his directors first thing in the morning and he still had a few hours preparation ahead. Something made him look back. Cassidy fingered her swollen lower lip as she stood in her doorway watching him. As their eyes met, he knew the promise he made to her in the car would be kept.

So that wasn't the reason for the churning in his gut. No, that was due to the fact that he knew the reason he'd made those promises wasn't because of his faith in their love but because he wouldn't be able to become CEO of Tolley-Patterson without Cassidy by his side.

He never lost focus, but right now he was torn. He wanted to stay with Cassidy even though he had reports to analyze.

He shook his head and got into the car. The job—his career at Tolley-Patterson—was the most important thing in his life. Winning the last challenge that Granddaddy had put before him and Sam was what he needed.

He glanced in the rearview mirror and saw Cassidy lean heavily against the doorjamb and knew he'd disappointed her.

Instead of going back, he hit the car phone button. "Call Marcus Ware."

"Calling Marcus," the car speaker responded.

Marcus answered on the third ring, exactly as Donovan expected of his right-hand man. Marcus had the same hungry ambition that Donovan did.

The other man lived for Tolley-Patterson and the deals they both made.

"Catch me up on where we stand with the West Coast production problem," Donovan said without exchanging pleasantries.

"Not good. Someone needs to go out there and take care of the problem. Jose's been trying to negotiate with the workers, but he's made little headway."

The last thing he needed right now was a trip to the West Coast. It was Wednesday, and he and Cassidy were getting married on Saturday. "Marcus, I'm getting married this weekend."

"I know, sir."

He'd informed his second in command of the marriage to make sure that he covered all the bases for the terms of the will. He'd instructed Marcus not to mention it to anyone yet. "I need this problem fixed tomorrow."

"That's why I'm booked on the next flight to San Francisco. I'm not going to leave the table until we have this dispute resolved."

"Call me when it's taken care of."

"I will."

He disconnected the call. Donovan knew that Marcus was ambitious; in fact, the younger man reminded him a lot of himself, which was one reason he'd hired him. He had brought Marcus up the ranks with him each time he'd been promoted, and if

Marcus got the West Coast operation back online tomorrow, Donovan intended to promote the man to his position when he became CEO.

And there was little doubt he'd be CEO with Cassidy already pregnant. Every detail was falling into place. So why then did he have this hollow feeling inside?

His cell phone rang and he glanced at the caller ID before answering it. "Hello, Sam. What's up?"

"My mother just called… So you're back with Cassidy Franzone." It was a statement, not a question.

"I am."

"You know that most of the board don't approve of her family."

"Granddaddy's will just said the CEO must be married and have an heir. It said nothing about the type of family she had to come from."

There was silence on the line.

"But I think everyone assumes you'll marry someone from Old Charleston."

"Then they don't know me very well, do they?" He deliberately didn't tell Sam that the wedding was already planned. No need to tip off the competition.

"No, they don't. But I do," Sam said. "You sound confident."

"I'm the best man to take control of the company, and at the end of the day everyone is more interested in making money than social connections."

Sam cleared his throat. "You aren't the best man for the helm, Donovan."

"You think you are?"

"I know I am, because I know that to be successful in business you have to have a life outside of the office. You have to see the world in which we sell our products."

Donovan disagreed, but then Sam had lost his competitive edge four years ago when he'd married Marilyn. Since then Sam had become strictly a nine-to-five man, getting home to his wife every night. Donovan knew that a lot of people believed in balance, but he thought that theory was full of crap.

"Well, we'll see what the board decides in January when they meet."

"Yes, we will. Good luck," Sam said, hanging up.

Donovan continued driving, needing some time to figure out if there was value to anything Sam had said. He'd kept the news about Cassidy's pregnancy to himself and he wondered if his mother had, too. She probably hadn't said anything about it to her sister, Sam's mother, because his marrying his pregnant girlfriend wasn't exactly something she'd brag about.

For the first time in years, Donovan thought about his dreams and he realized that home and family had never been part of them. And with Granddaddy dead, he didn't know what he was searching for anymore. The old man's approval was always going to be just out of reach.

Four

"I don't like the way he's come back into your life," Adam said.

It was the same argument she'd heard many times since she'd called her brothers to tell them she and Donovan were getting married. At least her mother was thrilled for her. Her father had been out of town on business at the time and had sent her a text note to say that he hoped the house would be repainted by the wedding day. She tried to pretend it didn't matter that her father was more concerned about business than her, but deep inside it did.

"You promised you wouldn't start anything today."

"I'm not starting anything, Cassie," Adam said, sitting down next to her on the settee and putting his arm around her. "I just don't want to see you hurt again."

"I'm not going to be hurt again. Raising my baby with his father is what I've wanted since I found out I was pregnant."

"I don't understand why he left in the first place," her other brother, Lucas, said as he joined them. "And now he's back."

Eight months ago, she hadn't told her family that Donovan didn't want kids. She'd kept that to herself because it had been such a deep blow. Now she realized that they must have guessed anyway from the way the relationship had ended.

"It wasn't about the baby," she said.

"Of course not," Lucas said. "It was about him not being ready to be a father."

Lucas was married and had three sons. He had been a father since he was twenty-one and at thirty he felt that he was an expert on what men should do in family situations. Adam was three years older than Lucas and married to his job.

Her brothers had a lot in common with Donovan in that they seemed to exemplify the fact that men could be either family oriented or workaholics. Especially if their work involved a family business.

"Could be. Not every man is like you. Just

because he needed time to consider everything doesn't mean anything."

"Having a wife and kids isn't an easy thing for some men," Adam said. "I couldn't do it. The job comes first for me the way it does with Dad."

Lucas nodded. Cassidy remembered every event their father had attended for them when they were growing up. Because there had only been two events—Adam's graduation from prep school and Lucas's college graduation. Their father had always put business first.

She put her head in her hands. The things that Donovan had said since coming back into her life made her believe that he was truly a changed man. That he was really going to be in her life and their child's.

Could she do what her own mother had? Could she watch her children's disappointed faces as their father once again missed out on an important school function?

"I need to talk to Donovan."

"Now? Why? Are you having second thoughts? We'll go and tell him the ceremony is off," Adam said, standing up and heading for the door.

"Adam, no. I just want to talk to him."

"Beth had the jitters on our wedding day," Lucas said. "Of course, our situation wasn't that different from yours."

Lucas's wife had been pregnant at their wedding—not as far along as Cassidy was, but pregnant all the same. "Are you happy, Lucas?"

"You know I am. But it was a struggle at first."

Lucas came over and hugged her close. "He wouldn't have asked you to marry him if he didn't want to make the relationship with you and your baby work."

She nodded. Lucas was always the sensible one. He'd made family his number-one priority, working a low-stress job so he could coach his kids' Little League team and be at every school event.

"Can you guys leave me alone for a few minutes?"

Lucas gave her another hug and then nodded. "Let's go."

Both her brothers left the room. Cassidy went to the French doors that led out to the garden, which had a beautiful white gazebo in the middle that overlooked the ocean. Chairs were set up for the few guests, and flowers decorated the white lattice around the sides of the gazebo.

The backyard looked fairy-tale perfect. Like something out of *Bride's* magazine—if you ignored the fact that the house in the background was bright pink. And Cassidy wanted to believe in the picture-perfect image. But she was a realist. Picture-perfect was just an image, not reality.

Not knowing exactly where Donovan was at this moment, she went to the house phone and dialed his cell number. While the phone rang, she tried to think of what she'd say, how she'd word her questions. The words eluded her.

"This is Donovan."

"Hey, it's me."

"Hello, baby. Is everything okay?"

There was caring and concern in his voice, bringing up her usual dichotomy of feelings toward Donovan. He was like this sometimes, and then she remembered the way he'd kissed her with all that passion and left her on her own doorstep.

Did he have a switch inside that he turned on and off when it came to her? How would having a father who did that affect their child?

"Cassidy?"

"I have to ask you something. I'm not even sure what I want you to say, but it's important, okay?"

"Sure. Go ahead."

"What kind of a father are you going to be? I mean, are you going to always be at work when our son has a school event, or will you take time off for him?"

"Just a second." She heard the scrape of a chair and then the ringing of his footsteps on a hardwood floor. He must be in her father's study. A second later she heard a door close, and then he said, "I don't know."

"Oh."

"Cassidy, less than a week ago I found out I was going to be a father. I came to your house that night planning to ask you to be my wife, but beyond that I haven't had time to think about our son."

"But just thinking about it now, what's your gut reaction?"

She heard him take a deep breath. "My gut is to tell you what I know you want to hear. But lying to you, Cassidy, isn't something I want to do. I have no idea what kind of father I'll be. I do know that I want to know our son and be a part of his life, but work has always been my focus... I can't promise to change that, but I can promise I will try."

She held the handset loosely and thought about what he'd said. "I'm not going to let you fail at this, Donovan. My dad...he wasn't there for us growing up. Now he's trying, but it feels like guilt. I'm going to insist you be a part of your son's life."

"Good," he said. "We'll make this life of ours work...together."

Donovan glanced over the small crowd of people gathered in back of the Franzones' gaudy pink mansion to celebrate his marriage to Cassidy. Tony Franzone was standing off to one side talking on his cell phone. The man was a better father than Cassidy realized—he'd come over to Donovan earlier and told him in no uncertain terms that if Donovan made his daughter cry again he'd put a hurt on him. The man had actually said that.

Donovan understood the sentiment that went behind it. He searched the crowd for his own parents and found them sitting alone, not talking to each other but each staring at the people around them. He saw his mother shudder when she took in the Franzone mansion.

His extended family had never been close-knit, and he didn't think they ever would be. He told himself it didn't matter that family had no place in his life and they'd never been particularly close, but a part of him was disappointed that more of his relatives weren't here.

Of course, he hadn't invited that many of them. He'd needed to keep the marriage quiet until he was ready to talk to the board.

Marcus had resolved the West Coast matter on Thursday and was back in the office Friday. Donovan had gotten a late-night call from his uncle Brandt congratulating him on taking care of the mess. Brandt had hinted that marriage was the only thing keeping Donovan from the CEO position. Donovan had almost told his uncle about the wedding, but had decided discretion was still wise at this point.

Donovan steeled himself as Adam Franzone approached.

"You sure about marrying my sister?" Adam asked as he came to stand in place next to Donovan at the stairs of the gazebo.

"As sure as any man can be," Donovan said.

"Hurt her again and I'll make sure you regret it for the rest of your life."

"I didn't hurt her on purpose eight months ago. I proposed to her, and she turned me down."

"She turned you down?" Adam asked.

"Yes, she did." He knew now that she had done it because of what he'd said about not wanting a family. From what Adam said, he must have hurt her. "I'll take care of Cassidy."

"Make sure you do."

"Are you threatening me?" He knew he'd do the same if he were Cassidy's brother and some other man had abandoned her. It was a sobering thought, and for the first time he was forced to look outside of himself.

"Yes," Adam said, totally unashamed of himself. "I should have done it the first time you dated her. I knew you were the kind of man who always put himself first."

"The same can be said of any successful businessman. And that's what women want, Adam. Success."

"They also want a guy to be able to balance that with family time."

"I don't see a ring on your finger. What makes you an expert?"

"The fact that I don't have a ring. I've spent my entire life avoiding the situation you're in because for me work always comes first."

Donovan knew it did for him, too. Always had. That was why he'd let Cassidy go. Because he'd known she could interfere with his success.

Donovan didn't want to have this discussion with Adam. The pressure he was under at work to make sure that every aspect of his division was running smoothly was tremendous.

"If it were any other woman, I'd walk away," Donovan said, realizing the words for the truth they were. It didn't matter that he'd had Granddaddy's will as an excuse to get back to her side. He'd wanted Cassidy for a long time. And now that he had her back where she belonged—in his life—he wasn't going to let her go.

The music started and Donovan saw Emma walking up the aisle. And then, Cassidy. She looked so lovely that for a second his breath caught in his throat. He was humbled by the fact that she was marrying him and having his baby.

Humbled by the fact that this woman was now going to be his. When she got to his side and he took her hand in his, he saw the joy on her face and knew he never wanted to disappoint her.

She could never know that he had come back into her life because of a will. That he was marrying her not only for herself but also because his job demanded it.

The lie of omission weighed on him. He would have to balance it with his actions. He was marrying her, and that was ultimately what she'd always wanted. And he would do his damnedest to be a good husband and father. But part of him—the man who was her lover—knew that Cassidy was never going to see a lie as balanced out by anything.

As he took her small hand in his and turned to face the pastor, he vowed to himself that he'd make their life together so fulfilling that, if she ever found out the real reason he'd come back to her, it wouldn't matter.

As the pastor led them through the ceremony, he felt the noose tighten. He heard words he'd heard a hundred times before in other ceremonies, but this time they sank in. This time they resonated throughout his body. His hand tightened in Cassidy's, and she looked up at him.

"You okay?" she mouthed.

He nodded. But was he? Marriage wasn't something to be entered into lightly. And this was the worst possible time for him to be having this thought, but maybe marrying Cassidy wasn't the only solution.

Then the pastor asked if he took Cassidy to be his, and the panic and the uncertainty left. Cassidy was already his, and this ceremony today would do nothing but affirm that to the world.

"I do," he said.

Cassidy smiled up at him, and that was it. That moment of panic retreated to a place where he would never have to think about it again. He wasn't a man who looked back and lamented the choices he'd made. He was a man who looked forward and shaped his own destiny, and this moment, with this woman, was where he was meant to be.

The rest of the ceremony passed in a blur and before he knew it, the pastor was telling him he could kiss his new wife.

He pulled Cassidy into his arms, felt the bump of her belly against his stomach. As he lowered his head to hers, she came up on her tiptoes, meeting his lips. He stroked her mouth with his tongue before pushing inside. She held on to his shoulders and he bent her back over his arm, kissing her and claiming her…Cassidy Franzone—no, Cassidy Tolley. His wife, his woman, the mother of his child.

"Cassidy, do you have a minute?"

"Sure, what's up?"

"I just heard something… I don't want to make waves on your wedding day, but—"

"Emma, just say it. Whatever it is."

"Um…there's something weird going on with Tolley-Patterson."

"Like what?"

"I don't have the details, but one of the attorneys at my father's firm, Jacob Eldred, handled Maxwell Patterson's will. I was talking with some of the firm's associates at a cocktail gathering the other night, and when I mentioned I was attending your wedding, they said something about Maxwell's will."

"His grandfather's will?"

"I couldn't ask more. I started to, and then they realized that they shouldn't be talking to me about the matter, so I asked my father, but you know how he is."

Cassidy sat down and Emma sat next to her, holding her hand. "I…I don't know what to think."

"I know, Cassidy. It may just be business, but I was thinking about how he came back to you out of the blue…."

"I don't think our marriage has anything to do with his job. His grandfather liked the fact that Donovan was single."

"You're right. I just wanted to mention it."

"Mention what?" Donovan asked, coming up behind them.

"Nothing, Donovan. Just a comment I'd heard about you and your grandfather's will."

Cassidy wasn't sure, but it almost looked as if Donovan's face went white. "Like what?"

"Nothing specific, just that it was a bit strange."

"Well it's one of those old-time Southern wills. Nothing either of you has to worry about."

Emma and Donovan had never been great friends. She wished they'd find a way to get along, but it wasn't a main concern of hers. They didn't have to be best friends for her to continue her relationship with each of them.

"Of course it isn't. That's business and this is personal," she said to Donovan. Donovan reached for her hand and she gave it to him. He drew her to her feet. "Did you need me for something?"

"I wanted to dance with you," he said. "Will you excuse us, Emma?"

Her friend nodded, but Cassidy sensed that it wasn't over. There was more to what Emma had been saying, and she'd talk to Donovan about it later. Tonight, she wanted to enjoy their party. To hang on to the illusion that he was her Prince Charming and she was embarking on happily-ever-after with him.

The band started to play "Do You Remember" by Jack Johnson, and Cassidy tipped her head back. "Did you request this?"

"I did. I couldn't think of a better song to be our first as husband and wife."

She'd always liked the song. It had a feeling of

permanence to it. A feeling that the couple would be together forever. And she'd always wanted that for her and Donovan.

"I didn't think you'd remember I liked this song."

"I remember everything about you, Cassidy."

Sometimes, when he said things like that, she knew that her doubts about him were groundless. He drew her closer and sang along with the lead singer. His voice made her feel good deep inside.

She loved being in his arms. She'd missed that so much. She sighed and snuggled closer to him. His hands smoothed down her back and he shifted a bit to pull her even closer.

"Baby, you okay?"

"Yes. I've missed your arms around me."

"Me, too," he said. "We'll never sleep apart again."

She liked the sound of that. But she knew he traveled for business and doubted the words were the absolute truth.

She'd thought that getting married today would ease some of the doubts she'd been carrying inside, but instead she realized that more were being generated.

"Don't you want that?" he asked.

"Yes. I've missed sleeping next to you."

"I'm hearing some hesitation in your voice."

"There isn't any. I was just thinking how our lives sometimes don't follow the path we want for them."

"Even me?"

"Especially you."

"What can I do to alleviate those fears?"

She shrugged. "I don't know. I worry about a lot of things lately."

"What did Emma say to you?" he asked as the band switched gears to play an old Dean Martin song, "Return to Me." She suspected one of her brothers had requested it, since it was her parents' wedding song.

"Something about your grandfather's will."

"What about it?"

"Just that it was a bit strange," she said. "Don't my mom and dad look sweet?"

"Your mom does."

"Dad's not that bad. I'm just glad he was able to make it today. They were having some problems with the workers' union."

"Your dad's a tough guy, and he doesn't look sweet at all. I'm glad he made it today, as well."

"With Mom, he always seems different."

"He loves her," Donovan said. "That's why he's different."

"Yes, he does. Even when Dad disappointed us, he would never disappoint Mom."

"That's not a bad thing, Cassidy. He probably did what he could to be a good father to you."

"I know. I'm not complaining. It's just that if he'd

been the way he is with Mom with me and the boys…"

She didn't know that it would have made a difference. But she thought about Adam and how he was sure he couldn't be a father and an executive, and then she thought about how Donovan was going to be both.

Donovan was a man who never let anyone get the better of him. Not her, not his cousin, not a business rival. What kind of father was he going to be? Someday, were they going to be dancing together at their child's wedding, or would they be divorced… two strangers standing across the dance floor, remembering this moment when they were young?

"Cassidy?"

"Hmm?"

"Don't worry about anything. We're together now, and that's all that matters."

She wished she could believe him, but a part of her feared that just being together was never going to be enough for her.

Five

Cassidy had envisioned her wedding night many times when she'd been younger. Now, looking at herself in the mirror of the bathroom dressed in a maternity negligee, she felt…scared. She'd made love with Donovan many times, but he hadn't seen her body since she'd been pregnant.

And she wasn't even sure that she could make love to him now. Her stomach felt tight, and she couldn't stand still. Probably because of worry over what Emma had said to her. What did she really know about why Donovan had come back?

Only what he'd told her.

Did she trust him? Heck, she already knew that

she did trust him, now she just had to let go of the past and her fears and simply enjoy being with him.

He knocked on the door. "Are you almost done in there?"

"Yes. Just washing my face," she said, turning on the water to give her lie credence.

She heard the door open behind her and leaned down to cup her hands under the water, but then she froze. Donovan had removed his shirt and had on only his dress trousers. They hung low on his hips.

He looked incredibly sexy and she wanted nothing more than to get closer to him. To wrap her arms around his lean waist and rest her head against his chest and pretend that all the things she was worried about didn't exist.

"Why are you hiding out in here?"

"I'm not hiding. I just want… Okay, I am hiding. You haven't seen me all pregnant before. And this is our wedding night, which is supposed to be romantic, and I'm not sure I feel romantic at all."

"That's fine. Just come out and let me hold you," Donovan said.

He opened his arms and she stepped into them. The baby kicked as he drew her close, and Donovan's hand moved to her stomach, resting on the spot where the baby's foot had just been.

Donovan lifted her into his arms and carried her out of the bathroom and across the luxurious hotel suite to the king-size bed. He set her gently in the center of the bed.

He followed her down, lying next to her on his side. He propped his head up on his hand and stared down at her with a look of concentration.

"You seem very serious."

"I'm lying here with my wife…."

Her husband. She hadn't really let herself believe it, no matter how many plans they made, because a part of her hadn't been sure they'd get to the altar. Being married quietly with just family in attendance had sounded good when she'd insisted upon it, but now it made their relationship seem like a secret. That, and the fact that he hadn't wanted to put an announcement in the newspaper about the marriage.

"You're thinking way too much," he said, leaning down to trace her brow with one fingertip.

"Donovan—"

His mouth on her neck made her stop. She didn't want to have a heavy conversation tonight. She wanted just to lie in his arms.

She put her hands on the back of his head, felt the silky strands of his hair against her skin. His breath was warm against her, his mouth a hot brand as he kissed her neck.

She shifted onto her side and into his body. With a hand on her hip he pulled her closer and raised the fabric of her nightgown up over her legs.

"Lift up."

She shifted her hips and he drew the nightgown over her head. And she was lying there completely bare except for her panties. He traced a path from her neck down over her breasts, which were bigger now than they had ever been before. Her nipple beaded as he drew his finger around the full globe of one breast.

He bent to capture the tip of her breast in his mouth. He sucked her in deep, his teeth lightly scraping against her sensitive flesh. His other hand played at her other breast, arousing her, making her arch against him in need.

He lifted his head. The tips of her breasts were damp from his mouth, and very tight. He brushed his chest over them.

"Is this okay?"

"Yes," she said, feeling cherished by the gentle way he was touching her.

"I want you, Cassidy."

She slid her hand down his body and wrapped her fingers around his erection. "I know."

"You are so damned sexy. I've been thinking of this moment all day."

"Have you?"

"Mmm, hmm," he said, his mouth on her breast again. He kissed his way lower, following the mound of her stomach. He paused, whispering something soft that she couldn't hear.

He shifted on the bed, kneeling between her legs, and caressed her body from her neck, down her sternum to the very center of her.

"Do you want me?"

"Yes," she said, shifting her legs on the bed.

He drew her flesh into his mouth, sucking carefully on her. His hands held her thighs open, his fingers lightly caressing her legs as he pushed her legs farther apart until he could reach her dewy core. He pushed one finger into her body and drew out some of her moisture, then lifted his head and looked up her body.

She watched as he lifted his fingers to his mouth. "I've missed your taste."

Donovan had always been an earthy lover, and she hadn't realized how much she'd missed their lovemaking until this moment.

He lowered his head again, hungry for more of her. He feasted on her body, carefully tasting the flesh between her legs. He used his teeth, tongue and fingers to bring her to the brink of climax but held her there, wanting to draw out the moment of completion until she was begging him for it.

Her hands left her body, grasped his head as she thrust her hips up toward his face. But he pulled back so that she didn't get the contact she craved.

"Donovan, please."

He scraped his teeth gently over her and she

screamed as her orgasm rocked through her body. He kept his mouth on her until her body stopped shuddering and then slid up her.

He wrapped his body around hers. "That will have to do until after you have my baby. But you know that I've claimed you as my wife."

"Claimed me?"

"Yes. I don't want there to be any doubts. You are mine, Cassidy Tolley, and I don't give up anything that is mine."

Donovan woke aroused. He wanted to make love to Cass, and as she shifted against him he thought she was feeling the same way. He pulled her more fully against him and she turned her head into his shoulder, moaning softly.

He leaned down to find her lips. They parted under his and he kissed her. He knew he couldn't pull her under his body as he would have in the past. He skimmed his hands down her curves. Her hands tightened on his shoulders and her eyes opened.

"Hey, baby."

"Hey, you," she said, shifting in his arms and kissing him lightly.

He leaned in to kiss her again when she drew back. And groaned this time. "Donovan?"

"Yes."

"I think my water just broke."

"What the hell?!" He jumped out of bed, glancing around for his pants. He found them on the back of the chair. He wasn't completely unprepared for this. He'd had his assistant get him a couple of books on pregnancy, and he knew the layout of the hospital where Cassidy was expected to give birth…in two more weeks. He was even scheduled to attend his first childbirth class with Cassidy next week.

"Did it?"

She glanced down at the bed. "Um…yes."

He kept cool but inside he was panicking. What was he supposed to do with a pregnant woman? "Okay, let's get you dressed and we'll head out."

"Donovan?"

"Yes, baby?"

"I'm scared."

"Don't be. I'm here and I'll make sure everything goes exactly the way it's supposed to." He knew then that he couldn't give in to the uncertainty that swirled around him. He had to be the one to take control and present a calm front for her.

She smiled at him and he felt the burden he'd taken from her. He was scared, too, because he didn't want anything to go wrong. He needed Cassidy, and not just because he wanted to beat Sam in their quest for the CEO position.

He grabbed clean clothes for her from her overnight bag and called her doctor while she changed in the bathroom. He finished dressing and got his wallet. He also called the valet desk and had them bring his car around.

The door opened and Cassidy stepped out looking a bit dazed and scared. He didn't think of anything but Cassidy and the baby. Didn't think of anything but taking care of her.

This was a first for him, putting someone else completely before himself. He'd analyze that later. But for now, as they were riding in the elevator, he just wrapped his arm around her and held her close.

"I was so sure I could do this on my own," she said.

"You could have. Your mom would have been here with you, or Emma."

"That's true, but I was just thinking that having you here is exactly what I need. With you I can really relax and know that you'll take care of everything."

He really was a bastard for having walked out of her life the way he had and for only coming back for himself. There was so much he hadn't realized he was doing to her.

His car was waiting when they got downstairs and Cassidy started having some serious contractions while he drove them to the hospital. The decision to have their wedding night in Charleston instead of somewhere else outside the city had been a good one.

"Did you call my parents?"

"Not yet."

She pulled her phone from her pocket and dialed their number. He half listened to her conversation, thinking about the fact that this was his life now. This woman and the child about to be born.

He wasn't sure he was ready for his life to change this drastically.

He pulled into the parking lot at the hospital and got Cassidy out of the car and into the reception area. He pushed aside everything but Cassidy and the baby. He took control in the waiting area, got the nurses to see to Cassidy. He signed paperwork and talked to the doctor on call. Then there was nothing else to do.

He paced around the private room. It was nice enough, he supposed, with walls painted in neutral, soothing colors.

"Stop pacing," Cassidy said.

"Sorry. After all the stuff we had to do to get here, just standing around waiting for the monitor to do something…"

"Is making you crazy?"

"Pretty much. The next thing that should happen is your contractions getting more intensive. I'll help you manage them."

"You will? How?"

"By managing…distracting you," he said.

"I'm not exactly looking forward to this part," Cassidy said.

"What did you think when you found out you were pregnant?" he asked.

"Well, at first I was excited."

"When did you find out?" he asked. Everything had been going so fast since he'd walked back into her life that he hadn't had a chance to really talk to Cassidy about the baby. He'd been at the office as much as possible, shoring up his position with the board. Making sure that they knew he was the only man for the CEO position.

"The day you asked me to marry you," she said.

He crossed his arms over his chest. "Why did you turn me down? I mean, you knew about the baby, right?"

She closed her eyes for a second, and he checked the monitor and saw that she'd just had a contraction. "Sorry about missing that."

He went back to her side and took her hand in his. He kept one eye on the monitor. "Tell me why you didn't just marry me when I asked you to. Was it only because of what I said about children and family?"

"Yes. I didn't want you to feel trapped. I could have mentioned I was pregnant, and I know you, Donovan, you would have done the right thing."

He wasn't too sure about that. As much as he prided himself on being an upstanding man, a real gentleman when it came to women, he'd also seen what kids did to a man and his career. Relationships that had once been solid often folded under the pressures that a man inherited when he became a father.

"What's wrong about that?" he asked, truly not understanding what she was saying. He only knew that if she backed out of being married to him now, he didn't know what he'd do.

"I wanted you to marry me for me."

Cassidy didn't want to have a conversation about herself right now. The baby and marriage weren't exactly topics that she wanted to discuss during labor. She was interested in finding out what was going on with his cousin and Tolley-Patterson, but right now she didn't think she was up to an in-depth conversation.

Right now, she was figuring out that moderate pain wasn't as moderate as the books described—or maybe she was wimpier than the average woman. Hell, she didn't care. The sensation in her abdomen was getting more intense and Donovan was standing over her, looking like a man who wanted to discuss the weight of the world.

"Baby," he said in a very low tone, and she felt a sting of tears in her eyes.

She turned away so he wouldn't see. He sounded as though he really cared. The man who could never and probably would never tell her how he felt had a voice that could melt her heart sometimes. She hated her weakness for tears. Especially now, when she was trying not to let him see how much pain she was in.

"I was speaking hypothetically. I was a man who arrogantly thought he knew what he felt about children."

"And you didn't?" she asked. Because Donovan was the kind of man who knew how he stood on every topic. She appreciated that he wanted to make her feel better and was trying to say something that would, but she saw through his words to the truth underneath.

And that truth was exactly what she'd feared. That Donovan would have married her and in fact probably *had* married her because she was pregnant with his child.

"Well, let's just say that I didn't anticipate anything to do with you and me and this child."

"What does that mean?" she asked, feeling her stomach start to tighten.

"You've got another contraction coming," he said, holding her hand solidly in his.

She gripped his hand.

"I just… Listen, Cassidy," he said once her pain subsided. He sank down on the bed next to her hip and took her hand in both of his. "My life was on a certain track, you know? Working my way to the top and proving to Granddaddy that I was his logical successor was always my focus."

He was trying to tell her something, but she had no idea what. There was too much going on inside her as her body prepared to give birth. She appreciated that Donovan was finally opening up to her but now was seriously not the time.

"I know. You've always been focused on your job," she said.

Her belly started to tighten again and she clamped down on his hand, her nails digging into his skin. "God this hurts."

Donovan held her hand through the long contraction and then stood up. "I'll take care of this."

She was amazed at how quickly he got the floor nurse into her room to take care of the pain. The technician who was supposed to be administering her epidural arrived and in a very short time she was resting comfortably. Donovan was commanding and in charge, making sure the hospital staff took care of her every need.

Her mother and Emma arrived. The women swarmed around the bed to ask if she was okay. Her father stood in the hallway, cell phone attached to his ear. She could hardly believe he'd come at this hour.

"I'll leave you alone with your girls for a little while. Have them call me on my cell if you need me." Donovan kissed her forehead.

She nodded, guessing he was uncomfortable and

probably needed his space. But the last thing she wanted at this moment was for him to leave. She was scared that something would go wrong with the labor or that Donovan wouldn't get back in time to be by her side when she delivered.

"Where are you going?"

"Just down the hall. I want to call my parents," Donovan said.

"You'll be close by?" she asked.

"Yes," he assured her. Leaning down, he brushed the bangs off her forehead. "Emma?"

"Yes."

"You come and get me the moment anything changes in here. I want to be by her side."

Again she felt that melting deep inside. That certainty that Donovan had the same deep emotions for her as she did for him.

"If she wants you, I'll come and get you," Emma said.

Donovan kissed Cassidy again and left the room. Her mom and Emma both stood there for a second.

"Tonight?" Emma asked, a grin teasing her features. "On your wedding night you go into labor...that has to be the best wedding-night story ever."

"I don't know about best, but certainly the strangest."

"Oh, no, not the strangest," her mom said. "Cousin Dorothy's husband had an allergic reaction to the silk of her negligee and his entire body was covered in hives. He had to be rushed to the E.R."

Cassidy laughed at the story and once she started she found she couldn't stop. Soon her laughter changed to tears and she was crying.

Emma held her left hand and her mother leaned down to hug her from the right side. "Everything is going to be okay."

"Promise?"

"Yes. Childbirth is the greatest experience a woman can have."

"Greatest?"

"Cassidy, you are taking part in a miracle. You are going to be holding your son in a few hours and all of this will be forgotten."

Cassidy liked the sound of that. But then, her mother had always known how to say the right thing at the right time. She held tightly to Emma's hand and realized that as much as she appreciated her mother and her best friend being with her, she really needed Donovan.

She was afraid to ask Emma to go get him. Didn't want to seem too needy on this night, especially after she'd told him she hadn't wanted to be married for their child.

But when the door to her room opened a while later and Donovan poked his head in, she felt relieved. "Do you need anything?" he asked.

"You," she said.

Six

Cassidy woke from a sound sleep in a panic. Nearly three weeks had passed since she'd given birth and returned to her new home with Donovan and their baby boy. She glanced at the clock, and that only intensified her feelings. It was nearly 9:00 a.m. And Donovan Junior, or Van, as they'd decided to call him, hadn't woken her. She jumped out of bed and grabbed her robe on the way out the door.

She ran over the marble floor to the nursery door, which was closed. Who had closed the door? Her son wasn't even a month old, no way was she going to close the door to his room at night.

She pushed it open and stopped still in her tracks.

Van's crib was empty, and on the changing table were his pajamas. But no baby.

She walked back out to the hallway and made her way down the stairs. Hearing the sound of Donovan talking, she went to his home office and stood on the threshold, peering inside.

Van was in Donovan's arms, dressed in a pair of khaki pants and an oxford cloth shirt. He looked like a mini Donovan in his work-casual attire. Except that her son was drooling a bit as he slept.

The sight of the two of them, her two men together, made her heart stop. She just stared at them. And felt all the worries she'd had since her Donovan had come back into her life fade. Seeing him holding their son was all she'd ever wanted.

He looked perfectly at home with Van. Donovan had the baby cradled on his shoulder while he paced the room, talking to the speakerphone.

"Joseph has asked for a special board session to discuss Van."

"He can convene the board as often as he wants. Until the official board meeting, no changes can be made," Donovan said.

"He's positioning himself for the official meeting. There is only three months until the vote. And I have to tell you, what I'm hearing doesn't look good for you."

"Let me worry about my position, Sam. I've

heard the same things about you. Marcella isn't too happy with the way you've been handling the Canadian Group."

"You barely pulled the West Coast office through the latest mess."

"But I did. And that's what the board is looking for."

"You know, Granddaddy isn't here to set us against each other anymore."

"He left us one last challenge, Sam."

"And you think you won?"

"I know I did," Donovan said. Turning around, he paused as his eyes met Cassidy's.

She took another step into the room.

"I'll call you back, Sam."

He leaned down and hit a button on the phone.

"What was he talking about? Why does the board need to talk about Van?"

"It's nothing for you to worry about. Did you enjoy sleeping in this morning?"

"Yes," she said. "Though I did panic a bit when I woke up so late and couldn't find him."

"You have lunch today with Emma and Paul, so I figured the little man and I could spend all day together."

"That's very thoughtful," she said. She walked over to Donovan and kissed Van on his head. She hadn't known it was possible to love another being as much as she loved her son. Having him put every-thing in perspective. There was nothing in the world that was as important as taking care of him. She'd been disappointed when breastfeeding hadn't worked out for them, even though it gave Donovan more ways to help with his care.

"Are you sure you'll be okay with him?"

"Yes," he said. His cell phone rang and he glanced at the caller ID before turning back to her.

"Do you need to get that?"

He shook his head.

"Good. I've been wanting to talk to you about Sam and Tolley-Patterson… Emma heard some rumors about an odd stipulation in your grandfather's will."

"That's confidential information."

"She didn't know the details, just had heard a comment at a cocktail party her parents had." Cassidy had tried to bring up the will a few times, but she'd been tired from giving birth and taking care of her son. She hadn't really had time to investigate it further until now.

"From who?"

"Lawyers at her father's firm," Cassidy said. "Emma mentioned it because…"

"She was hoping to stir something up between the two of us," Donovan said.

"True, and I trust you, sweetheart. I'm just worried Sam might be putting together something shady.

And what I heard just now makes me even leerier of him."

Donovan hugged her to his side with his free arm. He kissed her. "Don't worry, baby. I've got everything I need right here."

"Really?" She was afraid to believe him when he said things like that. She knew that his life was business and everything else came second.

"Yes."

She tipped her head back and leaned up on her tiptoes to kiss him, but he dropped his arm and stepped away and she stood there awkwardly for a second. Donovan and she hadn't been out together since they were married, and he worked long hours. In fact, this moment was the most waking time she'd spent with her husband since they'd left the hospital.

She wasn't sure what was going on in his mind. Did he regret marrying her? They could have just as easily had Van and raised him without being married or even living together.

"What?"

"Nothing."

"Not nothing. You were staring at me like you wanted to say something."

She did, but how was she going to ask him if he no longer found her attractive since she'd given birth? How was she going to bring up the fact that she needed more one-on-one time with him?

"Just wanted to follow up on our plans for today. Are you sure that you can take Van this morning?"

"Yes, I can."

She stared at Donovan and realized that the love she'd always felt for him was getting stronger. She wanted him to be the husband she'd always fantasized about, and he was doing some things that made her believe he was that man. But then there were times like just now, when he'd pulled back from her, that let her know this wasn't a fantasy happy-ever-after marriage, but one based on necessity and reality.

Donovan wasn't the type of man who'd ever cared to be domestic, and carrying Van into the office didn't change his mind. The secretaries all cooed over the baby and the other men stood kind of awkwardly to one side while he set the baby in his car seat on the boardroom table.

"Never too early to start training the future generations," Marcus said as he entered the room.

Donovan laughed. "That was my granddaddy's creed. My earliest memories are of Sam and I playing on the floor of the executive offices."

"And now you're passing it on… I never saw you as the kind who'd bring a kid to work."

Donovan hadn't, either. He still wasn't one hundred percent certain of himself as a father or in the father role. But being in the office energized him, raised his confidence. Here he made no missteps. Here he knew exactly what he was supposed to do and how to do it.

As opposed to at home with Cassidy, where he was stymied by his own desire for her. It was all he could do not to make love to his wife. He knew she needed time for her body to recover from giving birth, but he was constantly aroused when he was around her.

This morning he'd woken up with a hard-on and had started to caress her when Van had cried out, stopping Donovan from making love to his wife.

"Let's get on with this meeting. I'm not sure how long Van's going to sleep."

"Don't you have a nanny or something?"

"Not yet. Cassidy is still interviewing them." Donovan didn't see how that was Marcus's business. He had the right to have his son with him in the office.

Marcus raised one eyebrow and shook his head. "This is why I always keep things casual."

"Why?"

"Look at you," he said, gesturing to Van's car seat, which Donovan had positioned directly next to him. "Your attention is divided now."

Donovan didn't like the way that sounded and glanced protectively at Van. Van was the future…his future. And he wanted his son to know from the start that he loved and cherished him. It was important to Donovan that Van feel comfortable in the offices of Tolley-Patterson and not as if he had to compete for the right to be there. "Have a seat, Marcus."

"Yes, sir." Marcus sat down as the rest of the staff started filing in.

Donovan moved Van's car seat to the credenza that sat against one wall, close enough so he could see his son but far enough away that the meeting wouldn't disturb the baby.

He brought the meeting to order, but his mind was only half on business. The other part was on Van. The baby had simply been a tool to beating Sam to the final prize his grandfather had dangled in front of both cousins. But now, as he watched his boy sleeping, he realized that the baby was so much more to him. Everything.

Marcus had been right on the money when he'd said that Donovan had changed. How had that happened? It seemed as if he'd become a different man. How could a few short weeks change a man's life?

"Donovan?"

"Yes?"

"We were discussing the budget for the next quarter... Do you think we're going to need an increase in labor on the West Coast?"

Donovan pulled himself back into the meeting, pushing little Van to the side of his awareness, but it was hard. And as he tried to focus on the business at hand, he realized it wasn't just Van who was on his mind, but also Cassidy. He remembered her earlier kiss and how he'd gotten hard just from holding her. He could hardly think from wanting her.

He knew they still had a few more weeks before he could make proper love to her. And yet his body didn't seem to care. He wanted her. He needed to seal the bond of their new life together by thrusting into her sexy body and making them physically one.

He hardened thinking about the way her mouth had felt under his and her warm body had felt pressed against his side.

Was that why he was distracted? Because he hadn't been able to make love to his wife? He scrubbed a hand over the back of his neck, trying to release the tension he felt. But cold showers weren't working, and a quick massage wasn't getting the job done.

The only thing that would take care of his problems was Cassidy.

He suspected that this was what Marcus had been referring to. The need he felt to be with her every minute of the day. The way she was infiltrating this meeting without even being in the room with him.

The meeting adjourned thirty minutes later and Donovan picked up Van and went toward his office.

"Theo is waiting in your office," Karin said when he reached the outer office.

"Was he on my calendar for today?"

"No, but he wouldn't take no for an answer. He said it was highly urgent, regarding the upcoming board meeting."

"Okay. Anything else?"

"A few messages, I left them on your voice mail. And Sam wants five minutes of your time to discuss Canada."

"I talked to him at home this morning. When did he call?"

"Twenty minutes ago."

"Very well. When Theo leaves I'll call him."

"Do you want me to keep Van while you meet with Theo?"

Donovan set the baby seat on the edge of Karin's desk and set the diaper bag next to it. "Do you mind?"

"Not at all. My kiddos are all teens now, I miss little ones."

He left Van with Karin and entered his office. There was a sculpture in the corner that his father had made for him when he'd gotten the promotion to executive vice president. The desk that he used had been his great-grandfather's.

"Afternoon, Uncle Theo."

Theo was currently serving as interim CEO until the next board meeting when either Sam or he would take over that position. Theo was a bit of a cold fish and had at one time wanted to be appointed CEO, but he had given up that aspiration when Granddaddy had announced that either Donovan or Sam would be his successor.

"I'm not here for chitchat, Donovan."

"Why are you here?" he asked as he took a seat in the leather executive chair. He saw the picture of himself, Cassidy and Donovan that Emma had taken of the three of them in the hospital. Cassidy looked radiant as she looked down at their son and Donovan's stomach knotted thinking about how happy she looked.

In that picture they looked perfect, like a couple who'd finally made their lives complete by bringing a child into the world. Only Donovan knew the truth—that their life together was based on a lie.

"The board isn't pleased with your engagement to Cassidy."

"Engagement?" he asked. Surely his mother had told the other members of the board by now that he and Cassidy were married. She'd never kept anything from the board before. And even though he'd told her he wouldn't be announcing the marriage yet, he hadn't specifically asked her to keep it quiet.

"Yes. We understand that you want to marry her

for Van's sake, but we strongly recommend you end all relations with Cassidy Franzone and find a proper woman to marry."

Cassidy enjoyed her lunch with Emma and Paul, but seeing them together underscored the distance between her and Donovan. She knew there was something missing from their relationship.

"So how's motherhood?" Emma asked when Paul went to get the car and they were both alone.

"Good. Tiring, but good."

"How's marriage?"

"Um…"

"Not good? What's up?"

"Nothing really. It's just that I don't see Donovan at all. And when he is home, I'm exhausted."

"That's to be expected, given how suddenly you two married. What about at night in bed?"

She looked at her friend. Only the fact that Emma was the sister of her heart allowed her to even think of sharing.

"I'm usually asleep by the time he comes in, and if I'm not he just rolls over on his side."

"He might be afraid to touch you since you had Van. A lot of guys don't really know when it's okay to do that."

"This is Donovan we're talking about. He knows everything about…well, everything."

Emma pulled her compact and lipstick from her purse and touched up her lips. "I don't know what to say. Have you talked to him about it?"

"No." When she and Donovan had first started dating, he'd told her how much he loved her body, that her slim figure was one of the first things he'd noticed about her. Now she was afraid that her post-pregnancy belly was a huge turnoff for him. As soon as her doctor had OK'd it, she started doing sit-ups like a Marine going through boot camp, but her stomach had a little saggy bit that remained.

"That's what I'd do."

"Would you really, Emma? You wouldn't just let things ride to kind of keep the peace?" Cassidy asked her friend.

"Are you kidding me? There is never peace between Paul and I. We're always on about something."

Cassidy knew that. Emma's personality was a bit fierce and she didn't hesitate to speak her mind no matter what the circumstances. "What if you were afraid that you'd be bringing up something that would make Paul leave you?"

Emma nibbled on her lower lip. "Honestly, Cassidy?"

Cassidy nodded as she pulled her sunglasses from her Coach handbag. She hid her eyes behind the overlarge Gucci glasses.

"I'd do it. I'd probably be bitchy about it the whole time, though. I hate feeling unsure, you know?"

"Yes, I do. This entire relationship with Donovan has gone from nothing to everything in such a short span of time, I don't think I've had a chance to adjust." She hated how much she worried about everything with Donovan. Before, she'd known that she could make things right between them in bed, and now...that simply wasn't the case.

"He might be feeling the same way. I mean, he came back to you to try again, not expecting to have a baby and a wife so quickly. How is he adjusting to fatherhood?"

"I'm not sure. This morning he took care of Van so I could sleep in, and he does spend at least a half hour every morning with Van, talking to him and walking him around the house while I get ready."

"What does he say?"

Cassidy didn't know. She felt as if she was intruding and wanted to let Donovan have some alone time with their son. She knew the things she talked to Van about were personal. Things that were full of her love for her baby. And sometimes she talked to him about her dreams for him.

"Do you know?" Emma prodded her.

"Not really. But he does seem to be making time

for Van. I mean, he's a busy executive and that's not going to change, but when I need him he's there."

Emma gave her a one-armed hug. "He's different than I thought he would be at this point. I don't know what happened when ya'll were apart, but he's not the same guy he was before."

That was what she kept telling herself. And a part of her was afraid to believe it. She wanted this new beginning to be what led them to happily-ever-after. But she knew she was steeling herself for the possibility that it might not work out. And that attitude was coloring everything, making it so much harder to just be happy in the moment.

Maybe because she was afraid to let herself believe in those dreams that she'd held for so long.

Paul pulled up but was on his cell phone so Emma gestured that she'd be another minute. "He talks so loudly when he's on that thing."

Cassidy laughed at that. Paul did talk loudly on his cell.

"Did you ask Donovan about Maxwell's will?" Emma asked.

"Yes. He said it wasn't a big deal. He's already aware of whatever it was that Sam was talking about."

"That's all he said?"

"Yes. Why, did you hear anything else?"

"No. I asked my father about it, but he said it was none of my business."

"Well he's right."

"He isn't. If it concerns Donovan then it concerns you and we're best friends."

"Uh-huh. Did that change your dad's opinion?"

"Absolutely not. But he can be a bit of a stickler when it comes to rules. Remember that time he went ballistic when we took his Mercedes for a test-drive?"

Cassidy did indeed remember the incident, which had happened when they'd both been thirteen. Emma's older brother, Eric, had been bragging about his abilities behind the wheel and Emma had had to prove she could drive as well as he did. To be fair, Emma was at least as good a driver as Eric. Unfortunately her father didn't care about that, he cared only that thirteen-year-olds weren't supposed to be behind the wheel.

They parted ways when Paul got off the phone. Cassidy left, wondering if she had let her reunion with Donovan change something essential inside of her. She'd never been a coward before this. From the moment she'd met Donovan she'd known she wanted to be his wife—why would she let anything intrude on her happiness now that she was?

She needed to take some action. No more waiting for Donovan to make the first move. Tonight, when he came home from work and Van was in bed, she was going to seduce her husband.

Seven

Donovan drove home with Van buckled in the backseat of his Porsche Cayenne. He'd bought the SUV the day after they'd brought Van home from the hospital. The Cayenne had the engine power he was used to in his Porsche 911, but the safety and room needed for an infant.

He hadn't met with Sam or anyone else after Theo had left. His family made the Machiavellis look like inhabitants of *Mr. Rogers' Neighborhood*. He was angry and frustrated and ready to take on the entire board. This mess was getting out of hand. Grand-daddy had started this fiasco with his ridiculous will and the way he'd always pitted his sons and grandsons against each other.

He dialed his parents' number and got their housekeeper, Maria, who informed him that his mother was out for the evening with her bridge club and that his father was in his studio.

Without thinking twice Donovan drove to his parents' house. He needed to talk to his father. He took Van out of the car seat when they got there and found that the baby needed his diaper changed. Donovan took care of it and then carried the baby around the back of the mansion he'd grown up in to his father's studio.

He knocked on the door but then opened it and entered, knowing his father never answered the door. His dad held up one hand in a gesture that Donovan knew meant he'd be a minute.

So he took Van on a walk around his father's studio, showing his son the pictures that had been taken of his father at different exhibits.

"What can I do for you?" his dad asked.

"I'm not sure. Uncle Theo visited me today and warned me against marrying Cassidy…. Dad, what's up? I thought for sure Mom would have mentioned the wedding to more of the family."

His dad wiped his hands on the front of his shirt and then walked over to where Donovan stood.

"I have no idea. Your mother votes my shares and

has the active seat on the board. I haven't said anything to anyone because I've been in the studio. I have a show in three months and really don't have time for any of the Tolley-Patterson business."

It was a familiar scenario. Donovan had never really had any of his father's attention or his father's time. Sculpting came first for his father, and then family.

He looked down at little Van sleeping so quietly in his arms.

"I remember when you were that size," his dad said, gesturing to Van. "I used to keep you in here with me during the day."

He didn't remember that. "Really?"

"Well your mother was still an active executive at the company so it made sense for me to keep you. I had a playpen for you over in that corner."

His father turned to look in the direction he'd indicated and Donovan stood there awkwardly, realizing that he and his father had never been close so he'd never considered that he might have had dreams for him to be an artist. He thought of it now only because he knew he wanted Van to follow in *his* footsteps and one day take over running the family company.

"I need to talk to Mom about this. Will you ask her to call me when she gets home?"

"Yes. What did Theo say?"

"That I needed to marry a proper girl. One from the right sort of family."

His dad chuffed. "Sometimes I think the Tolleys forget that they were carpetbaggers."

"Dad, watch out, that kind of talk will get you disinherited."

"Wouldn't be the first time that I was threatened with that. That might not be a bad thing. Always remember that you aren't a clone of your grandfather."

"I know that."

"Do you? I think you've always wanted to be better than he was, but you know he took the company from a nearly bankrupt run-down business to where it is today. He carved his own path, Donovan, and I think a part of you has always hungered to do the same."

"Did he want you to do that, too?"

"We had a big argument about it when I decided to go to the Art Institute of Chicago instead of Harvard. He said that I was letting him down by not following in his footsteps…called me weak."

"That sounds like Granddaddy. He never could understand anything that happened outside the walls of Tolley-Patterson."

"I told him I wasn't his clone and I couldn't follow his path. I needed to follow my own."

Donovan's family didn't just live in Charleston, they were steeped in the history of this town. He'd grown up surrounded by his past the same way his dad had. But instead of shunning what was all around him, Donovan had embraced it.

Today, though, he'd seen another side of being a Tolley, and he acknowledged that Uncle Theo and the board might never come around to accepting Cassidy.

He left his father's studio with nothing resolved and more questions in his own mind. Had he been just as guilty as Uncle Theo and the board of discriminating against Cassidy and her family and friends? He had kept their marriage quiet so that he could use her and Van to the best advantage when it came to beating Sam.

He sat in the front seat of the Cayenne and glanced over his shoulder into the backseat. Van was awake and waving his fist in front of his face.

"What do you think, buddy?" he asked the baby. "Should I tell the board to go to hell?"

The baby cooed and looked up at him with eyes that were shaped like Cassidy's. He knew he had his answer. The thing was, he didn't know if he could let go of the goals that had been a driving force in his life for so long. Could he give up beating Sam and taking over as CEO for Cassidy?

Not that she would ask him to. But if his family wouldn't accept her, he couldn't allow anyone to treat her with disdain. All she'd ever done was love him and give him a son.

He leaned over to brush the drool off Van's lower lip with his thumb and realized that his life had already changed, whether he wanted to admit it or not.

Cassidy was ready for Donovan that night. She'd gone to the salon to get her legs waxed. She'd taken a long bath and taken time with her appearance. She'd gone shopping after she'd left Emma and purchased a new wardrobe that fit her postpregnancy body.

She'd even cut her hair and had it highlighted. She looked more like her old self than she had in a long time. She *felt* more like her old self. She glanced in the mirror and saw the flirty woman she used to be.

Cassidy gave the housekeeper the night off and was prepared to fix a simple supper of grilled salmon and watercress salad whenever Donovan got home. She even had a shaker and ingredients ready to make martinis as soon as he walked in the door.

She heard his car in the back driveway and realized she was standing around, staring at the back door as if she were waiting for him. Which she was, but he didn't need to know that.

But she had no idea where she should go. She didn't watch TV and the study was on the other side of the house. Dammit. Why hadn't she planned this part better?

She went into the living room to the wet bar and started mixing the drinks.

"Cassidy, we're home. Where's Mrs. Winters?"

She went over to Donovan and gave him a kiss on the cheek before taking Van from him. "I gave her the night off. I thought it would be nice to have a family night."

"Sounds good. We need to talk anyway."

"About what?"

"My family… What were you making here?"

"Gin martinis."

"I'll do that. Are we doing dinner?"

"Yes. Salmon steaks on the grill and salad."

He grinned at her and she felt the groove she'd been searching for between them. "I'm going to go change Van out of his work clothes."

"I'll come with you. I need a change, too. Is the baby too small for the pool?"

"To be honest I have no idea. I think he'll be fine as long as we hold him."

They walked up the curving staircase in the front of the house. Donovan touched her shoulder and then caught a strand of her hair. She turned and looked at him eye to eye since she was a step higher than he was.

"I like your hair."

"Thank you," she said, her voice sounding a little hoarse to her own ears.

"God, Cassidy, you are so gorgeous." His mouth found hers and he kissed her the way she'd been longing for him to. His lips moved over hers with surety, his tongue teasing first her lips and then brushing over the seam of her mouth and thrusting inside. He tasted faintly of mint and something that she associated only with Donovan.

She leaned toward him, wanting to feel his chest pressing against her breasts, but instead felt Van's little hand on the bottom of her neck. She pulled back and stared at her husband for a long moment, remembering the orgasm she'd had on their wedding night. Man, that felt like a lifetime ago.

Donovan kissed the baby's hand and then walked around her on the stairs and continued up toward the master suite. "He was good for me today. Slept through two meetings and flirted with all the secretaries."

"Then he's a lot like his father."

"Funny. You don't get to the executive office by sleeping through meetings."

"But flirting helps?" she asked, teasing him, trying to find some kind of lightness to take her mind off of the physical ache she felt. Oh, how she wanted him.

"It doesn't hurt."

They entered the master suite and Donovan went into his closet, to change, she supposed. She laid

Van on the center of their king-size bed. She took off his khaki pants and button-down shirt and then checked his diaper, which was dry.

The baby lay on his back cooing and chewing on his fingers until she handed him a little plastic pretzel chew toy. She wanted to go change but didn't feel safe turning her back for even a second while the baby was up on the high bed.

She took the bolster pillow from the head of the bed and put that on one side of Van and then used the other pillows to create a barricade around the baby. He wasn't crawling yet so he should be fine, she thought.

Her bathing suit was in the dresser in this room. She grabbed it quickly and then went back to the side of the bed. Van had fallen asleep in the midst of the pillows, the toy on his chest. She watched him as she got changed next to the bed.

Instead of the daring bikini she used to wear, she donned a new tankini, and when she caught a glimpse of herself in the mirror she thought she looked pretty good.

She turned back to Van, leaning over him to adjust one of the pillows. She felt Donovan's breath on the back of her neck a second before she felt his lips on her skin.

He nibbled down the length of her neck. She shivered under his touch as his hands found her waist and he drew her back against his body. His chest was bare and felt wonderful as he wrapped his arms around her and pulled her fully against his body.

"Can we make love?" he asked. "Because I'm aching to be inside you."

"I can't take you," she said. "Not yet. But in a few more weeks I can."

"Then we'll have to do something else, because I can't keep my hands off you for another day."

Cassidy turned in his arms. "I want you, too."

"I know."

She arched one eyebrow at him. "How?"

"Your pheromones have been making me crazy since I walked in the door."

She started to respond but he kissed her mouth, cutting off her words and making it impossible to do anything but kiss him back.

Donovan couldn't keep his eyes or his hands off Cassidy as they prepared and ate dinner. Van was sleeping happily in his portable crib and for a moment Donovan felt that everything in his life was perfect. There was none of the intense competitive need to be better than anyone. To keep reaching for that elusive whatever that was always missing in his life.

Instead, as he looked across the table at Cassidy sipping her pinot grigio and wearing that bathing suit, he felt something close to contentment. And that scared him as nothing else could. Content men weren't hungry or successful. Content men sat on the sidelines while others made things happen, and Donovan knew he could never be the kind of guy who did that.

He wanted Cassidy, wanted this peace she brought to him and his life, and yet he knew that this was false. That there was no way they were going to have this moment for too much longer. His job was going to come between them.

She had her iPod plugged in to the Bose speaker system that surrounded the pool and the songs that were playing were romantic. After holding her and kissing her earlier, he wanted nothing more than to make love to her.

But he needed to talk to Cassidy. Needed to tell her that most of his family didn't know they were married. He needed to come clean about what had been going on.

Part of him didn't want to. That was work related and shouldn't be something for her to worry about. This marriage was what she'd wanted. And he was going to make everything at Tolley-Patterson work out.

"You're staring at me."

"Am I?" he asked.

She nodded. "Why?"

"Because I want to."

She arched her eyebrows at him. "Why do you want to?"

One thing that had always drawn him to her was the way that her eyes sparkled when she laughed or teased. It wasn't even just when she teased him. He found her joy of life attractive no matter whom she was teasing.

"I'm surprised someone with your upbringing would do something as rude as staring."

"Well I'm a rebel."

"I've always liked that about you."

"What else do you like about me?"

"Your butt."

That surprised him and he leaned back in his chair. "I like yours, too."

"I know," she said, mimicking him from earlier.

The music changed and "Brown-Eyed Girl" by Van Morrison came on. Donovan was pushing back his chair as Cassidy got to her feet. "This is my song."

He knew that. It was always Cassidy's song. With her vibrant brown eyes and her shorter hair dancing around her shoulders, she started to move to the song. And he knew that, no matter what he'd been telling himself, this brown-eyed girl was important to him. At least as important as Tolley-Patterson.

He took her hand in his and drew her into his arms. She sang a bit off-key as they danced around the pool. Her limbs were silky and cool against his as he held her.

She tipped her head back. "I've been afraid of being myself with you."

"How do you mean?"

"Our marriage felt like it was so rushed, and I'm still not entirely sure why you came back when you did…." She pulled out of his arms. "I guess that part of me didn't want to rock the boat."

"I can understand that. I've been doing the same thing. Just working and keeping to my old routines."

"That's it exactly, but because I'm not working I've been sitting at home stewing and going a bit crazy because I couldn't figure out what was going on with you."

"And now you have me figured out?" he asked, sliding his hands up and down her back. It never ceased to amaze him how small she was or how right she felt in his arms.

"Not you. I figured *me* out. I was lost for so long, not sure what I was going to do, just waiting for Van to be born so I could figure out my next move. But now he's here and you're here, and I had to get here, too."

Listening to her talk made him feel like a bastard. He was here not because of any great philosophical development but because he needed her. "I didn't journey to you like that."

"It doesn't matter. This isn't about you really."

"Should I be offended?"

She shrugged. "If you want to be."

"Nah. Tell me more about being afraid to be you," he said. The music changed to Jamiroquai's "Virtual Insanity." And as Cassidy danced around him, he realized that she was a bit buzzed. She smiled at him each time she turned to face him.

"I think I didn't know if you could still want me, because I'd changed so much as a woman."

"In what way? By being a mother?"

"No. I mean my body. I've put on some weight and I'm never going to have that flat stomach I used to have."

He pulled her to a stop. "I love your body, Cassidy. Flat stomachs don't attract me—you do."

She tilted her head to the side and eyed him with that level stare of hers. The one that he was sure could see straight into his soul. "Really? The first thing you complimented me on was my slim figure."

"That's only because I thought I'd sound ridiculous if I told you that I loved your laugh and the way you smile when you're teasing."

She quieted and got really serious. "Do you mean that?"

"I don't say things I don't mean."

She wrapped her arms around him and squeezed him so tightly that he felt it all the way to his soul.

"Being married to you has made me so incredibly happy."

She rested her head on his shoulder and he held her loosely because he desperately wanted to clutch her to him. And men who were afraid to lose what they held were a liability. They stopped looking to the future and only looked to the present, his Granddaddy used to say. Those kind of men were the kind that life left behind.

Eight

Cassidy was seated at her vanity table when he came into their bedroom from putting Van down in his crib. He set the baby monitor on his nightstand and tried to calm his raging libido. Traditional sex was out of the question; she'd said she couldn't for a few more weeks. But he wanted to make love to her tonight. To seduce her with his lips and hands and give her the concrete reassurances that he still found her attractive.

"Thanks for tucking Van in."

"You're welcome," he said, watching her in the mirror. He walked over to her and put his hands on her shoulders. Her skin was smooth to the touch—

he never got over how soft she was. She smelled sweetly of flowers.

He leaned in low to brush his lips over her shoulder. Her nightgown had spaghetti straps and he kissed his way toward her neck, moving that thin strip of fabric out of his way so that he dropped kisses on every inch of her flesh.

"Donovan," she said his name on a sigh.

"Yes, baby?" he asked.

She turned on the stool and twined her arms around his shoulders, drawing his mouth to hers. Take it slow, he told himself. But slow wasn't in his programming with this woman. She was pure feminine temptation. He lifted her from the padded bench she sat on and set her down on the vanity counter. He slid his hands down her back, finding the hem of her nightgown and pulling it up until he caressed between her legs. She was creamy with desire, and hot.

She moaned deep in her throat and he hardened painfully. He thrust against her, rubbing their groins together until he thought he was going to explode.

He slid the straps of her nightgown down her arms until he could see the tops of her breasts and the barest hint of the rosy flesh of her nipples. He lowered his head, using his teeth to pull the loosened fabric away from her skin.

Her nipples stood out against the cool air in the

room. He ran the tip of one fingertip around her aroused flesh. She trembled in his arms.

Lowering his head he took one of her nipples in his mouth and suckled her. She held him to her with a strength that surprised him. But shouldn't have.

Her fingers drifted down his back and then slid under the T-shirt he'd put on to sleep in. She tangled her fingers in the hair on his chest and tugged, spreading her fingers out to dig her nails lightly into his pecs.

He liked the light teasing of her fingernails. She shifted back away from him, and he kept his hands on her breasts. His fingers worked over her nipples as she pushed the shirt up to his armpits. He let go of her for a minute to rip the shirt off and toss it across the room. He growled deep in his throat when she leaned forward to brush kisses against his chest.

She bit and nibbled and made him feel like her plaything. He wanted to sit back and let her have her way with him. But there was no room here. No time for seduction or extended lovemaking.

He pulled her to him and lifted her slightly so that her nipples brushed his chest. Holding her carefully he rubbed against her. Blood roared in his ears. He was so hard, so full right now that he needed to be inside of her body. But tonight he'd have to focus on other things.

Impatient with the fabric of her nightgown, he

shoved it up and out of his way. He caressed her creamy thighs. She was so soft. She moaned as he neared her center and then sighed when he brushed his fingertips across the humid opening of her body.

She was warm and wet. He slipped one finger into her body, felt the walls tighten around him and hesitated for a second, looking down into her heavy-lidded eyes. She bit down on her lower lip and he felt the minute movements of her hips as she tried to move his touch where she needed it.

He was beyond teasing her or prolonging anything. He plunged two fingers into her humid body. She squirmed against him.

He needed to taste her *now*.

He dropped to his knees in front of her, kicking the vanity chair out of his way.

"What are you doing?" she asked, looking down at him.

"Taking care of you," he said.

She murmured something he didn't catch as he lowered his head and touched his tongue to her center. Her thighs flexed around his head and he thrust his fingers in and out of her warm body. Her hands tangled in his hair as he caught her sweet flesh lightly between his teeth and nibbled on her.

He guided her hands to the cool surface at the rounded edge of the table. "Hold on."

"Yessss…" she said. And then he heard those little

sounds she made right before she came. He felt her body tighten around his fingers and was careful to keep the pressure on until he felt her shake and tremble around him.

He stood up and braced his hands on the vanity, trying to catch his breath.

She reached for him and he pulled away.

"Donovan?"

"Don't touch me, baby. I want you too badly right now."

She reached between their bodies and took him in her hand. "Let me—"

"Not tonight," he said. "This night is for you. I wanted you to sleep in my arms knowing how much I want you and how attractive you are to me."

"Thank you," she said.

"You're welcome, baby."

Cassidy never felt as wanted as she did that night in Donovan's arms. He brought her to orgasm after orgasm, and only took pleasure for himself when Cassidy finally insisted that she needed to enjoy the sensuality of his body as well. She fell into an exhausted sleep wrapped in his arms. Cuddled up against his side with his body pressed to hers she found a strength and peace that came from him.

But that peace faded at breakfast when she read

an article in the business pages about her son's birth in which she was named as Donovan's former girl-friend. She read the article twice and learned a little more about the situation that Donovan was facing at work. The reporter speculated that either Sam Patterson or Donovan Tolley would be appointed CEO of Tolley-Patterson at the next board meeting in January.

Cassidy finished her juice while she waited for him to come down from getting ready for work.

She heard the phone ring and a moment later Mrs. Winters came in with the cordless phone. "It's your mother."

"Thank you," Cassidy said, waiting until Mrs. Winters left the room before she lifted the phone. "Hi, Mom."

"Did you see this morning's paper?" her mother asked. It was noisy at her parents' house. Loud music and the sound of her mother's treadmill vied for dominance.

"Just now."

"What's going on? Why does this article make it sound as if you and Donovan aren't married?"

"I don't know, Mom. Donovan's still upstairs getting ready."

"Your father is outraged…. I think Adam is going to call the editor of the paper."

"Don't let him do that, Mom."

"Why not?"

"Because I wanted to keep the marriage quiet."

"Cassidy…"

"I needed time to adjust to everything and I didn't want there to be any speculation that Donovan married me because I was pregnant."

"Who cares what anyone has to say?" her mother said.

"Donovan's family."

"They're too full of themselves. It shouldn't matter to you what they think."

"I know, Mom."

Her phone beeped, letting her know there was another call waiting. She promised to call her mother back as she switched over to the other call.

"Hey, girl, brace yourself before you open up the paper this morning," Emma said.

"I've already seen it." She really should have thought through the consequences of keeping her marriage to Donovan secret. She'd just wanted a quiet ceremony and time for them all to adjust to being a family. How weird was it going to be for Donovan when he realized that his uncle had lied to protect their secret? She knew that honesty was one of the cornerstones of Tolley-Patterson. They had a public mission statement that reiterated that value.

"Okay. So what's up?"

"Um… Remember how I wasn't sure if Donovan was being real with me when he came back and proposed?"

"Yes."

"Well, I asked him to keep quiet about us. I just didn't want Charleston society to see our wedding as him marrying me for the baby."

"Why not?"

Cassidy wrapped one arm around her waist. "In case he changed his mind."

"Oh, Cassidy."

"I know. This is a mess."

"What's a mess?" Donovan asked. "Van?"

He entered the breakfast room and kissed her on the head. "You okay?"

"Emma, I'll call you back."

She hung up the phone as Donovan poured himself a cup of coffee. How was he going to react to the article? From their time dating, she knew he hated for any personal information to make its way into articles about him.

"There's an article about you and Van in today's paper."

"Just me and Van?" he asked, reaching for the newspaper. She handed him the Business section.

"Yes. It mentions me as your former girlfriend."

"Who mentioned you that way?" he asked, flipping to the article.

"Theo Tolley," Cassidy said. She'd only met

Donovan's uncle once, and from the article she'd learned that he was the interim CEO until the next board meeting.

"Dammit. It's not the way it might seem to you."

"What's not? Your parents were at the wedding, right? I mean, I know I wanted to keep it quiet, but I didn't mean that you had to pretend that we weren't even together."

Donovan skimmed the article and then turned away.

"I'm not pretending we aren't together," he said.

"It's okay," she said. "I suggested we keep things quiet. I just had no idea how it would feel to read something like this. It makes me feel like I'm not even a part of our son's life."

"There's a news van in front of the house," Mrs. Winters said, entering the kitchen.

Cassidy didn't like the sound of that. "Where?"

"At the edge of the property."

Cassidy had a feeling that more than the business journalists were interested in their story. For a society as staid and steeped in tradition and history as Charleston's was, this was a scandal. Especially since Donovan's family and hers were like oil and water.

"This is crazy." The last thing she wanted was to have to deal with the media today. Last night had felt like a real beginning in her relationship with Donovan.

"I agree," Donovan said. "This is a huge mess."

"Yes, it is. This goes way beyond an article in the business pages. If anyone does a records search, they're going to know that we *are* married, and then your uncle is going to look foolish. I'm not sure what to do. I should call my father and tell him what's going on."

"Cassidy…"

"I'm sure you'll have a plan for this. But talking to the reporters is something my father is used to doing. He can help."

"Your father can't comment on this. You aren't to say anything to the media. In fact, no one in your family is."

"You're kidding, right?"

"No, I'm not. Call your folks right now, tell them to say nothing."

"Donovan."

"What?" he asked, impatiently. She knew he'd probably already moved on to the next order of business in his head, but no way was she going to call her parents and tell them what to do.

"We have a problem. I don't take orders, and neither does my family."

"Until we have this sorted out, you both do," he said, walking away.

Donovan's first call was to an old college roommate, Jamie, who worked for the local NBC affiliate in Charleston.

"You are one hot story right now," Jamie said. "The stipulations of your grandfather's will were just leaked."

Donovan stilled. "By who?" he asked, his legendary cold, calm reaction coming to the fore. He automatically prioritized the situation and knew getting the media off his back was number one. Talking to Cassidy…oh, man, that was going to take more time.

"I don't know. I just wanted to give you the heads-up."

"Thanks, Jamie."

"You're welcome. I don't suppose you have a comment…"

"Not right now."

He hung up and called his uncle. Theo was on voice mail, and who could blame the man. His grandfather's will wasn't the first to have the kind of stipulation it did, but no one on the board wanted the media or the world to know about it.

"What is going on?" Cassidy said as she entered his study.

She held Van in her arms, and she looked upset.

Cassidy took a deep breath and released it slowly. Donovan watched her and realized for the first time that his priorities were wrong. He didn't care what the board did or what the media knew. He needed to make this right for Cassidy.

"I think it'd be better for me to handle this," she

said. "I can say that I wasn't ready to talk to the press since I just gave birth and that your family, out of concern for me, kept quiet." She gazed at him. "What do you think?"

He was speechless. That Cassidy would take the blame for something that wasn't even her fault was beyond his comprehension. He had to act. He hadn't anticipated Theo going after Cassidy in such a public way. Donovan was going to have to go in front of the entire board to get to the bottom of this.

Judging by his mention of Cassidy in the paper, Theo was up to something, and the power play wasn't one that Donovan was going to respond to.

"I think that you're extremely generous, but you should let me take care of this," he said.

"Well, I think we should handle it together. I'm going to issue a statement so that it doesn't seem as if I'm ignoring the media."

Donovan didn't want the story to go any further than it already had. He needed to get Marcus on the phone and have his team meet him at the office. It didn't matter that it was a Saturday.

"No. You will not do anything of the kind," he said. He pulled his cell phone from his pocket and sent a text message to his staff. He looked back up to see Cassidy glaring at him.

"What?" he asked, distracted.

"Did you just tell me what to do? *Again?*"

"Yes, I did. And I'm going to continue doing it."

"Excuse me?" Cassidy asked.

"You heard me."

"You are acting like a…"

"Jerk? I know. But you aren't prepared to deal with reporters shouting questions at you. And you're too old to have your father do it. I'll take care of it for us. This mess—"

"Mess? Do you mean our marriage and our son?"

Cassidy was on the verge of breaking down. He saw it in her eyes and in the almost desperate way she was holding their son close to her.

"No, of course not. You and Van are the best things to ever happen to me."

The words were meant to bring her solace, but they resonated with him, as well. He did need Cassidy and his son.

The doorbell rang but Donovan ignored it. "I think it would be best if you and Van kept a low profile until I talk to my people. Please."

"Fine," Cassidy said shortly.

Mrs. Winters knocked on the study door. "Sam Patterson is here."

The last thing he wanted was to have Sam here, but in light of the will being made public, the two of them would have to address the stipulation together.

"I'll be with him in a minute. Ask him to wait in the conservatory."

"No," Cassidy said. "Show him in here. I'll go upstairs and leave you both to it."

There was too much left unresolved between the two of them. He hadn't come close to explaining anything to her, and it was only a matter of time until she found out the entire truth.

"Cassidy?"

"Yes?"

"There's something I have to tell you—"

Sam entered the room without knocking. He gave Cassidy a vague smile and turned to Donovan. "We need to talk."

"Not now," Donovan said.

"Yes, now. You and Cassidy can finish your conversation later. Tolley-Patterson comes first."

"Not today."

"Really? Well then, our conversation will be short," Sam said. "I guess this means I'll be the new CEO."

"No, it doesn't," Cassidy said. She turned to Donovan. "Talk to your cousin. We can finish our discussion later."

Cassidy walked away, and as he watched her go, he began to understand just how much he loved her.

Loved her.

Nine

"Oh my God. You aren't going to believe it, but Donovan needed you and your baby." Emma burst into the sunroom.

"What are you talking about?"

"That's the weird will thing. The thing I told you I heard at the cocktail party? Maxwell's will said that either Sam or Donovan would be his successor and left them both some very challenging business objectives to accomplish."

"Of course he did. That was what he always did with those two," Cassidy said. "And it makes sense that either Sam or Donovan take over. They're both young and have the drive and experience to take the company to the next level."

"I'm not arguing that. But there was one more thing in the will…the reason why there are news vans outside your door."

Cassidy waited. She felt a trickle of apprehension, because there *was* something that Donovan hadn't told her. Some secret he'd been keeping.

"They each have to be married and produce an heir before they can be appointed CEO!"

Cassidy was glad she was sitting down. She felt faint and her stomach knotted. She thought about the new bonds she and Donovan had forged last night, and she realized that he had just been playing his part. Doing what he thought he needed to do to keep her happy.

She had feared being married for her child, but had believed that he'd only do that out of a sense of responsibility. She'd had no idea that he'd stoop this low. She knew that his company meant everything to him, but he should never have married her without revealing this.

"Cassidy? Are you okay?"

"Yes, I'm fine," she said, but she knew that wasn't true. And yet it was. Because she'd loved Donovan Tolley from the moment she'd met him and he'd smiled at her. She'd loved him even though he always put his job and career in front of her. She'd loved him even though he'd left her alone all those months.

And finally, she thought, she didn't love him anymore.

Well, that wasn't true. She still loved him, but she finally had the proof she needed that *he* didn't love *her.* That he wasn't ever going to love her the way she wanted him to.

"I'm sorry," Emma said.

"What for?"

"Being the one to tell you. But I couldn't let you find out from some nosy reporter."

"Thanks, Emma. I did need to know this. What am I going to do?"

"Take Van and leave. Let Donovan know that he doesn't have a wife or heir as far as you're concerned. Get him back for what he's done to you."

"Emma...I can't do that."

"Why not? He obviously didn't care about hurting you."

Was that true? She didn't know, and right now she really couldn't figure it out. She only knew that she hurt so much she couldn't think of what to do next. She needed some space.

Her cell phone rang and she glanced at the caller ID. It was her mom.

"Are you going to answer that?"

"Not now," Cassidy said, hitting the ignore button

on the phone. She put it on the table and then reached for Van, pulling him into her arms. She tucked him to her and let the love she felt for him soothe her. But it didn't, completely. When she looked into his eyes, she was struck by how much he was a part of both Donovan and her.

That he was a part of the lies that she'd been telling herself for so long.

Emma was staring at her, and Cassidy knew she needed to do something. "Thanks for telling me everything. I'm going to…"

Do what? She wanted in that instant to make Donovan feel the same kind of pain she was experiencing. Because the more she thought about that article she'd read, the more she began to suspect that he'd deliberately kept quiet about their marriage, possibly to use it to his advantage when the time came.

"I'm not leaving you. We'll fix this. I think the first thing to do is—".

"Nothing," Cassidy said. "I want to see what Donovan's going to do next. I mean, he's had a plan all along and I want to wait until he gets to his final move."

"And then tell him it's all over?".

Cassidy thought about that. Essentially, they *were* all over. This was the kind of blow to a relationship that she couldn't fix. The only thing that would fix it would be for Donovan to love her more than he did his job. More than he did the one thing he'd always turned to and found solace in.

Her anger mellowed as she realized they were both trapped in this thing together, because Donovan couldn't change the man he was. And she didn't want to stop loving him. The only way they'd both be happy was if that happened.

Because Donovan was never going to love her, and she wasn't going to be able to endure the humiliation of knowing that he'd come back into her life and married her simply to beat his cousin to the finish line.

Emma watched her and Cassidy realized she had to start detaching herself from her emotions. It was time for her to seriously move on. Or at least create the illusion that she had.

Deep inside, where she kept those dreams of happily-ever-after alive, she wept, but on the outside she simply smiled and stood up with her son in her arms.

"Let's go out," she said to Emma. She wasn't about to hide.

Sam paced around Donovan's office. He'd always seen his cousin as an adversary, and nothing in either of their lives had ever really changed that. The few times they had worked together, they'd both done so in their own way and with their own agenda.

This situation was no different. They were never going to be friends. But when it came to Tolley-Patterson, he knew that they both would do anything to make sure the company prospered and its profits continued to grow.

"We need to find the leak. This kind of press leaves us vulnerable and the investors aren't going to be too happy with the fact that a wife and child are the main requirements for their new CEO."

"Indeed," Sam said. "I've got Kyle from my team using his contacts to try to locate the source of the leak."

Donovan nodded. He was going to check with Jamie later to see if he'd found out anything more on the media side.

"I'm going to ask Theo and the rest of the board to address this. I already sent a message to Franklin in PR. I had asked him to draft a press release in case this situation arose," Donovan said.

"Why did you do that?"

"Granddaddy's will was too sensational for someone not to talk about it. Cassidy's friend Emma already had heard some rumblings, so it was only a matter of time."

"You should have kept me in the loop on this."

Donovan shrugged. He probably should have, but the will had been one of the things that he and Sam had never seen eye to eye on. If they'd both protested it, they could have gone to the board and had it thrown out. But Sam had steadfastly refused to do that.

"It's too late now. Franklin will issue an official statement from the company, and I think you and I should say 'no comment.'"

"I've asked the board to schedule an emergency meeting for tomorrow afternoon to give everyone time to get into town. I think we should both be prepared to make an argument for a new CEO appointment. Theo isn't equipped to deal with this, and I think our investors are going to need some reassurance," Sam said.

"I agree. I've got two of my guys monitoring our competition to ensure we know what they're doing."

Sam cocked an eyebrow at Donovan. "I guess we're working together on this."

"Seems like it."

"Did you ever wonder why Granddad always set us against each other?" Sam asked.

"Not really. I imagine you and I were always competing. I can't remember a time when we weren't."

In college, he'd gone to Harvard and Sam to Yale. They'd both interned at Fortune 500 companies, Sam at a company owned by one of Maxwell's cronies, Donovan at another one. For every major moment in his life, Donovan realized he'd basically been alone.

He was simply better by himself than working

with others. And that was part of what made him leery of this current situation with Sam and the company.

"I don't know if I can work with you on this," Sam said. "My instinct is to go to the media and do my own thing."

"But that wouldn't be best for Tolley-Patterson," Donovan said.

"No, it wouldn't," Sam said a bit ruefully. "Do you ever wish we were just two normal guys?"

"Hell no."

Sam laughed. "I wonder if Granddaddy had any idea that our path to the chairmanship would go this way."

"Who knows? The old man was good at thinking through every variable. But I don't think he could have predicted what happened with Cassidy and me."

Sam leaned back in his chair. "I'm not so sure about that."

"What do you mean?"

"Just that one look at Cassidy and everyone could tell she loved you. And I think Granddaddy always wanted that for you."

Donovan wasn't sure what Sam was getting at, but he didn't want to discuss Cassidy or how she felt about him with his cousin.

Donovan took control of the discussion and soon had the feeling that even Sam knew he was the right choice to lead the company. They spent the rest of the day in his home office on the phone with the board and different investors, working together to assuage them.

"Thanks for all your hard work today, Sam," Donovan said as his cousin prepared to go.

"You don't have to thank me. It's my company, too."

"True, but after today I think we both know that I'll be taking the helm."

"How do you figure?"

"You heard Theo say that they refused to waive the stipulations from the will. And with the board all meeting tomorrow, I'm going to push for a vote for the new chairman. Clearly I'm the best candidate."

Sam got to his feet. "Keep telling yourself that. If I ask the board to postpone the vote or to consider the fact that my wife may now be pregnant…"

"Whatever you do, I think we both know that waiting isn't the best course of action. We need to take the stand as a company that we have a bigger story than Granddaddy's will, and the only thing bigger than that is a new CEO. And I'm the most logical choice," Donovan said. He opened the door to his office to show Sam out.

"Don't bother," Sam said. "I know the way."

Cassidy collided with Sam on his way out the door. She had Van strapped to her chest in a baby carrier and her arms were laden with packages from her and Emma's shopping trip.

He steadied them both and glared at Van. "I hope you know what you've gotten yourself into."

"What do you mean?"

"By having a child with a man who lives only for the company."

Cassidy wasn't sure what had happened, but she'd never seen Sam so hot under the collar before. Though she wasn't happy with Donovan right now, she wasn't going to talk trash about him with his rival.

"Donovan always does what he thinks is best for Tolley-Patterson because he wants what's best for his family."

Sam's eyes narrowed. "I can't believe you're defending him. You know he used you."

"How do you figure?"

"He came back to you to beat me. How does that make you feel? You're nothing more than a broodmare to an egomaniac."

He wasn't telling Cassidy anything she hadn't already figured out for herself. And though she was angry with Donovan for his actions, she wasn't about to condemn him.

"You're nothing but a bitter man who's afraid to admit that he isn't as good as the competition," Cassidy said, desperately trying to hold on to her composure. Sam had just vocalized everything that she'd been thinking for a long time.

She believed, just as Sam did, that Donovan had been using her. Probably from the very beginning when they'd dated over a year ago. Long before Van had been conceived and his grandfather's will had demanded an heir.

Even her realization that Donovan probably couldn't help being the way he was didn't change the fact that he'd lied to her. That he'd made her believe that he'd come back to her because of a change of heart. But she'd begun to comprehend that maybe she hadn't really loved him as well as she thought if she hadn't understood that his love and focus was always going to be on work. She *knew* that. She had known that forever.

"I feel sorry for you," Cassidy said at last, running her hands over the back of her sweet, sleeping baby. No matter why she and Donovan had come together, she had Van, and that counted for a lot in her book.

"Why?"

"Because you're so busy looking at Donovan and blaming him for your failures that you haven't looked at yourself. You're the only one who can control your actions."

"I could say the same of you."

"How so?" she asked, setting down her packages so she could remove Van from the carrier.

"You see him as you want him to be and not as he really is," Sam said. "Turn around and I'll unhook the carrier for you."

Sam's entire demeanor changed and suddenly he was the rather mild-mannered man she'd met a few times before. It was odd to think that he was the competition for Donovan, because personalitywise the two men were polar opposites. Sam was more easygoing and inclusive…more of a team player than Donovan would ever be.

Donovan was a loner. And that was something she should have realized a long time ago.

"I don't know if I trust you with my back turned."

"Look," Sam said. "I'm sorry I attacked you like I did. Seeing your son…he reminded me of a conversation I had with Granddaddy last Christmas."

"What did he say?"

Sam shook his head. "That we had to remember Tolley-Patterson was looking to the future. That we weren't going to be the last generation to run our family's company."

"Maybe that's why he was so determined that his next CEO produce an heir," Cassidy said. It seemed to her that Maxwell Patterson had wanted to control his grandsons for as long as he could.

"Perhaps. I *am* sorry for what I said. It seems as if you do know what you're getting into with Donovan."

She smiled and tried to appear confident. But she wasn't sure she'd pulled it off. Because to be honest, she had no idea what to expect from Donovan. "I guess."

"The rest of the family isn't going to accept your marriage, Cassidy."

"Why not?"

"Uncle Theo's quote in the business section... Did you see that?"

"Yes, I did."

"Well, he knows you and Donovan are back together. He's trying to push the two of you apart."

"Why?"

Sam shook his head. "I can honestly say that it has nothing to do with you."

"Who does it have to do with? Van? I'm not going to let your uncle or Tolley-Patterson be the focus of his life. I don't want him to grow up like that."

Sam smiled at her. "I can see that Donovan chose the right woman to be the mother of his children."

It was such a change from where Sam had been before that she almost didn't trust him. "Thanks, I think."

"Do you need a hand with your bags?" he asked.

"No, thanks."

"Good night then," Sam said, and he walked down to his Mercedes and drove away.

Cassidy watched him go, wondering desperately what she was going to do about both the mess that was her marriage and her son's future.

Ten

Donovan didn't leave his office until well after midnight. Even though he hadn't spoken to Cassidy, he knew she was aware that he'd married her to fulfill the requirements of his grandfather's will. Her lack of contact spoke volumes. He rubbed a hand over his eyes. They felt gritty and his back ached from sitting in one position for too long.

The house was quiet and air-conditioned cold as he walked up the grand staircase to the second-floor landing. One of his father's sculptures was displayed there. This one was of him, from when he'd been in his first year of college. The cold marble seemed startlingly like him. The eyes were vacuous, though, something he'd never noticed in his own.

Seeing himself in stone like this always made him strive harder. Work harder. His grandfather used to say that the boy in that sculpture had so much potential and fire to change the world. And Donovan was reminded of those words each time he walked past it.

But he was fifteen years older and he'd changed. He'd had to change. Hadn't he?

He entered the master suite and found it empty and quiet. He stood in the doorway feeling the hollowness of his victory. His long hours in the office this last week had assured that victory. Tomorrow there would be a public announcement officially declaring him the new CEO of Tolley-Patterson.

And he was all alone.

He strode to his nightstand and reached for the fine quality embossed note card that had Cassidy's monogram on the front. Not the one from when she'd been a Franzone, but the new one that reflected her married name.

He opened the card and traced his finger over her signature. It was flowery and pretty, very feminine and reflective of the woman she was.

Donovan,
    I hated to leave without saying anything but I couldn't wait around for you. I need to get

away so I can think about everything that's happened. I think I made a mistake in marrying you so quickly, without understanding exactly what your needs were.

Van and I are moving back into my house so I can have space to figure this out. I know you'll be busy with the company and your new role. Somehow, without even asking, I know you will be the new CEO.

I pray it's everything you hoped it would be.
Love, Cassidy

He tossed the note on the bed and left the bedroom. The house was a monument to his success. He had every "thing" anyone could possibly want. And for what?

He shook it off. Cassidy was just a woman. He'd lived just fine without her for the eight months they were apart. He went downstairs to the wet bar and poured himself a stiff drink.

He heard a sound behind him on the marble floor and turned to see a shadow in the doorway.

"Cassidy?"

She stepped into the room.

"I thought you'd gone."

"I did."

She wore a pair of faded jeans and a scoop-neck, sleeveless top. She looked tired. Her eyes were red, and he suspected that she had been crying. *He had made her cry.* He tried to think how he could make it better for her. She'd come back, so that had to mean that she didn't really want to be apart from him.

"Where's Van?"

"With my parents. I needed to talk to you. I want to make sure you understand why I left."

"I run a multimillion-dollar company. I think I can figure it out," he said, not really up to discussing all the things that were wrong with him when it came to relationships.

"You can be a real bastard."

"I know," he said, rubbing the back of his neck. "Listen, I didn't mean it that way. You know how I am. I'm not the kind of guy who talks about his emotions…."

He trailed off, hoping that she'd rescue him. That she'd give him a pass the way she had so often before. But she didn't.

"I do know how you are."

"Then why are you surprised?"

"Because…listen, I can't explain it any better than to just say I love you. And I think in loving you I made you into the hero I needed you to be. I have always been drawn to men who are driven, and you are that in spades."

"So what's the problem?"

"I thought you were different from my dad. That you had all of his strengths and none of his weaknesses."

"I've never talked on the phone all through a dinner with you."

"Donovan…do you care about this relationship, or do you want me to just walk out the door?"

It would be so much easier to have a clean break with Cassidy. She complicated things, complicated his life endlessly because she made him want to be that white knight she thought he was.

But he wasn't naive and never had been. He couldn't be the man she wanted him to be. His life was this empty house. His life was Tolley-Patterson.

"Donovan?"

"Yes?"

"What are you thinking?"

"About letting you go," he said honestly.

"That's funny," Cassidy said, feeling calm for once. No tears burned in her eyes. She felt nothing but a sense of unreality. "I think you probably already let me go…almost a year ago."

He shook his head and walked to her. He looked so tired and drained, and she wanted nothing more than to open her arms and offer him the comfort of a hug. But this was the man who kept breaking her heart, and solace wasn't something she should even be thinking of giving him anymore.

Yet to quit loving him was hard. She couldn't just fall out of love with him in less than one week. She couldn't stop the emotions that had been there from the moment their hands had touched. But she was determined to let him go. Determined to make a new start for herself. One where Donovan was nothing more than her baby's father.

"Baby, I have been holding on to you in ways you can't even imagine," he said.

The words sounded true, but she had learned during their brief marriage that Donovan wasn't above manipulating the truth.

"It feels to me more like you're pushing me away. You lied to me, Donovan. Flat-out lied when I asked you why you came back."

She'd come back for closure. Writing a note to him and leaving the way she had had left her feeling as if…oh, God, as if maybe there was still a chance for the two of them. The only way she was going to be able to move on was through some sort of final conflict.

"What did you want me to say, Cassidy? That I needed a wife and a baby for the company?" he asked, sarcasm dripping from every word.

"Well it would have been the truth." She wasn't about to take the blame for this. He had lied to her, and he had planned to keep on lying to her.

"You were happy to believe I was back for you."

"I was happy to believe that, because I wanted it so much. But I think maybe I was lying to myself. Listen, I just came back tonight because I didn't want things to end the way they did last time." She thought about telling him about her other stop that day—at his parents' house—and decided against it.

"I'm not sure what you mean," he said. "There isn't any reason for our marriage to be over...but that's what your note meant, right?"

"Yes. Our marriage *is* over." It was mainly pride talking, but she didn't care. She was tired of loving Donovan too much and him caring for her too little. She was never going to be able to compete with Tolley-Patterson. She was never going to be able to challenge him and fill his life the way that company did. She was never going to be anything more to him than the mother of his son.

"Why?" he asked.

He seemed perplexed, and frankly she didn't understand it. He had to see that she was more than a cog in the wheel of his plans for the future.

"What do you mean, why? Honestly, I think you can see why we can't stay married."

She wanted to say because he'd hurt her when he'd lied to her, but it was more than that. Tonight, as she'd tucked Van into his crib at her parents' house and seen the picture her parents had placed over his crib of her and Donovan holding the baby in the hospital—she'd wanted desperately for the emotions she felt to be real on both sides.

"No, I can't, Cassidy. Nothing's changed."

"Everything's changed."

He came over to her and took her hand in his, lacing his fingers with hers. She noticed the way their wedding rings nestled together.

"I married you, and we had Van together. My grandfather's will was in place before he was born."

"I didn't know that that was why you married me."

"Haven't you been happy?" he asked.

She *had* been happy. Had been finding her way in this new role. She still had to go back to her job, and they'd never made a public announcement of their marriage, but she'd been happy with Donovan.

"Well, yes, but…" How to explain? "I kept hoping you'd come back, and then you did. I set myself up for it."

"Set yourself up for what?"

She swallowed hard, hating to admit once again that she'd wanted to be wanted, to feel special, for herself. To be the one thing that he hadn't been able to live without.

"For you. I set myself up to be totally vulnerable to you. And that's what makes me mad. I made everything so easy for you."

Donovan cursed and dropped her hand, pacing

away from her. She watched his back, watched him walk away, though he didn't go too far. She made herself watch that view and remember it. He had walked away from her, and from her love.

"Nothing about this has been easy, Cassidy. Lying to you didn't sit right with me, but as long as you seemed happy I told myself that the ends justified the means."

"Of course you would say that. You've never needed me the way I need you."

Silence built between them, and she realized how much she'd hoped he would argue with her about this. Hoped that he'd suddenly confess to loving her and needing her. And the last of her dreams around Donovan Tolley died.

She pivoted on her heel and walked toward the door.

"Cassidy, wait," he said.

She stopped where she was but didn't turn around. The numbness she'd wrapped herself in when she'd come back to this house was fading, leaving behind the kind of aching pain that she'd experienced only one other time…when he'd let her down before.

"How can I fix this?" he asked.

That he'd asked made her feel marginally better. That he couldn't figure out what she needed from him negated those good feelings. No one wanted to have to tell someone that they needed to be loved. That they needed to be first in their life.

"I don't think you can."

There were a few moments in a person's life that defined him, and Donovan knew this moment with Cassidy was one. This would determine for the rest of his life what the balance of their relationship would be. And he had only to think about that feeling he'd had when he'd walked into the empty master suite to know that losing her now wasn't an option.

"*Can't* isn't in my vocabulary," he said.

She glanced back at him, that long curly hair of hers swinging around her shoulders. "What are you trying to say?"

He didn't blame her. He'd used evasion and half-truth for so long. They'd become his standard way of communicating with everyone. It was simply easier to play his cards close to his chest. He could protect himself and use the knowledge he collected to his advantage.

And the knowledge he'd collected about Cassidy was simple and straightforward. She needed some kind of emotional reciprocity. And it was about time that he delivered it.

But laying bare his soul…

"That we aren't done talking yet. Don't walk

away while there are still things to be said." No response. "Please."

She turned to face him, arms crossed. "I'm listening."

"Let's go outside. I'm tired of being in the house."

She nodded and followed him out onto the patio. The soothing sound of the waterfall in the pool area eased the tension that was riding him.

He didn't lose. He wasn't going to lose Cassidy. He just had to do the right thing. He'd always been able to fix things that way.

This was no different. He was going to win Cassidy back. He'd come back from worse situations. It wouldn't be the first time that he'd been down like this. She wouldn't have come back tonight if she hadn't wanted to.

"I know that I haven't exactly been your knight in shining armor, but I can change that. This stuff with Granddaddy's will was making me a bit crazy, and I had to focus on that and outplaying Sam. But that's behind me now, and I want to make you and Van the focus of my life."

Cassidy watched him and he didn't even kid himself that he had any idea what she was thinking. But he did know that she was no longer walking away. It eased the ache that he'd felt when he'd stared at her back.

"You're talking about starting over?"

"If that's what you want. I'd prefer to start from here," he said, meaning it. "We've had some good times, haven't we?"

"Yes, we have. But I can't—"

"What?"

"Listen, I want this to work. I mean, I love you, Donovan, but you have been a jerk about certain things in our relationship, and I'm not about to put up with it anymore."

"Fair enough. You tell me what you want me to change and I'll change it."

"It's not that easy."

"Why not? That's what makes the most successful relationships work."

"What relationships?"

"Business partnerships, mergers."

He felt her go quiet. She stopped leaning toward him and even though she didn't turn away he felt exactly as he had earlier when she'd walked away.

"Mergers? Was this a hostile takeover, or a friendly acquisition?"

"A friendly merger," he said, drawing her into his arms.

She held herself stiff and he realized that the situation was slipping away from him again. Was it time to pull back and regroup? Hell, he'd never done that and wasn't about to now.

He leaned down to kiss her but she put her arm

between them. "This will change nothing. Physical compatibility isn't the issue between us."

"Prove it."

"*Prove* it? You're supposed to be the one giving ground and wooing me back."

"Am I?"

"Yes," she said. "And frankly, I'm not that impressed right now."

He pulled her back into his arms and didn't hesitate to take her mouth. He kissed her slowly and deeply, reminding her with passion of the bond they shared. Reminding her that it was deeper and stronger than anything she'd experienced before. Than anything *he'd* experienced before.

He wasn't going to accept defeat. He swept his hands down her back to the curve of her hips, holding her tightly to him. Dominating her with the passion that had always been so much a part of their relationship.

She moaned, a sweet sound that he swallowed. She tipped her head to the side, allowing him access to her mouth. She held his shoulders, undulating against him. He wanted more of her and hardened in a rush. Making love to Cassidy was an addiction.

He brought his hand between them, cupping the full globe of one breast. She shivered in his arms as he brushed his thumb over her nipple.

He lifted his head so that their eyes met. Slowly he raised the hand between them and unbuttoned her blouse. She arched her shoulders and let him push the blouse off. She reached for the front clasp of her bra, opening it and baring herself to him.

He pushed back a little to see her. Her breasts were bare, nipples distended and begging for his mouth. He lowered his head and suckled.

He held her with a hand on the small of her back and buried the other in her hair. She arched over his arm, and her breasts thrust up at him. Nothing compared to the way she made him feel.

Her eyes were closed, her hips moving subtly against him, and when he blew on her nipples, goose-flesh spread down her body.

He loved the way she reacted to him. Her nipples were so sensitive he was pretty sure he could bring her to orgasm just by touching her there. He kept kissing and caressing, gently pinching her nipples until her hands clenched in his hair and she rocked her hips harder against his length. He thrust against her and bit down carefully on one tender, aroused nipple. She cried his name, and he hurriedly covered her mouth with his, wanting to feel every bit of her passion, rocking her until she quieted in his arms.

He held her close. Her bare breasts brushed his chest. He was so hard he thought he'd die if he didn't get inside her. Yet this was the perfect moment. Because he knew that he'd turned a corner, and that Cassidy was the one negotiation that he couldn't bear to lose.

Oh, hell, he loved her.

Eleven

Cassidy got out of bed late in the morning. The room was empty and it was clear that Donovan was gone. She dressed in last night's clothing, since she'd packed all of her other clothes the day before. She heard Mrs. Winters in the kitchen and smelled the enticing aroma of coffee wafting through the house.

She felt small and alone, ashamed that she'd let herself fall once again for Donovan's silver-tongued charm.

She was in the foyer when Mrs. Winters came out of the study. "Good morning, Mrs. Tolley."

"Morning."

"Mr. Tolley left this for you."

"Thank you." She took the small, oblong-shaped box and put it in her purse. She'd received enough jewelry in her life to recognize the box for what it was. And it felt like a bribe. She needed to get out of this house and back to her own.

She walked out of the house. There was a News 4 Van parked at the end of the circular driveway. As she approached her car, a reporter and cameraman scrambled toward her. She hated this part of being an heiress and a magnet for news.

Deciding she wasn't going to talk to anyone, she got into her car and put on her dark glasses. They ran toward her, but she waved them off and drove away.

But she had no idea where to go. Her parents' house, she imagined, was the best place. She called her mom to let her know she'd be there soon to pick up Van. She could collect her son and then plan a trip out of town for a few months. Until the local media had something better to report on than her and her Donovan.

When she pulled into her parents' house, her older brother, Adam, was standing in the portico.

"What are you doing here?"

"Waiting for you."

She stared at him, nonplussed. "How'd you know I'd be here?"

"I was with Mom when you called. I thought we should talk," he said, taking her arm and leading her to the back gardens.

"About?"

"Tolley-Patterson. It seems that the stipulation of marriage wasn't the only thing in that will of Maxwell Patterson's. He also left it up to the board of directors to approve Donovan's choice of wife."

"That's ridiculous."

"Exactly. I don't know what's going on today, but according to what I've been able to piece together, Donovan called for an emergency meeting to force the board to make a decision on the CEO."

"Why are you telling me this?"

"Because I have a man on the inside—"

"You sound like a secret agent, Adam. What does that mean?"

"A guy who works for Tolley-Patterson is keeping me abreast of what's happening in the meeting."

"Why would he do that?"

"I asked him to."

"Oh." No further explanation seemed to be forth-coming. "What did he say?"

"That the board will only accept Donovan as CEO if he doesn't marry you."

She heard the words as if from a distance and realized what they meant. Donovan had to choose between her and that position he'd always craved. Her and the last chance he had to prove himself to his grandfather over Sam.

"Thanks for letting me know."

"Cassidy?"

"Yes?"

"Mom and Dad have suggested having your marriage annulled quietly so that you don't have to go through the humiliation of a divorce."

She nodded. "Are they waiting for me?"

"Yes."

"I'm not going to let them take over. I need to do things in my own time."

"What will you do?"

"Talk to Donovan. Who's your source?"

Adam turned away from her. "I don't think I should say."

"I think you better. Is he reliable?"

Adam faced her again, taking off his sunglasses. There was a seriousness in her brother's eyes that she was used to seeing, but she also noticed that he seemed angry. She knew it was on her behalf, and she realized how deeply she was loved by her family.

"Very reliable."

"Who?"

"Sam Patterson."

"*Sam?* He hates Donovan! Adam, I wouldn't trust anything that he said. He's always working an angle."

"Hell, I know that. That's why I contacted him. I wanted to know more about what was going on."

"Why would he talk to you?"

"I have no idea."

"Liar."

"Liar?"

"Yes. You wouldn't make a deal with a man you didn't trust and there has to be more to this than Sam keeping you in the loop out of the goodness of his heart."

Adam looked uncomfortable for a moment before he put his sunglasses back on. "You're right. There is. I'm helping Sam with a contract he's working on in Canada using some of our contacts."

He didn't elaborate, which just made her mad. She was sick of the men in her life. Just plain sick of them and the way that everything in their worlds revolved around business.

"Did he say when we'd know what the board decides?"

"We should know soon. They're due for a lunch break in a few minutes."

Theo's power play was going to net Donovan the results he wanted. Donovan had no doubt about that. The board of directors had been unmoved by Theo's presentation, he suspected.

"What are you going to do?" Sam asked him as they both stood outside the boardroom. They'd been asked to leave while the board had a final vote.

"About what?"

"If they insist that you not marry Cassidy."

"Sam, I'm already married to her, so there's little the board can do. Even they can't insist I get a divorce."

"You're *married?* I thought she was just living with you."

"Do you honestly think I wouldn't marry her?"

"Well…yes. We all believed—"

"All? Who else? Theo? Have you been in league with him?"

"No. Theo has his own issues because Grand-daddy left him out of the running for successor."

Donovan agreed. Maxwell Patterson had left them all with a heck of a mess. The company wasn't in the best financial shape, but with him and Sam working as they had for the last few months, Tolley-Patterson was finally on the right track.

"If not Theo, then who?"

"Um…Adam Franzone."

"Then you must have known I was married to Cassidy," Donovan said.

"No, I didn't. Adam and I have a very limited agreement—I'm keeping him informed about what's going on in the board meeting today, and he's using his contacts to get us the land we need in Canada for our new facility."

Donovan was surprised that Sam had thought to use Adam for help in the land acquisition, which had been progressing very slowly. "Did you go to him?"

"No. Adam came to me."

Donovan realized that after all the years he'd spent competing with his cousin, he really didn't know the man. He had always just looked at Sam's weaknesses and tried to exploit them. But now he saw a glimpse of a future.

"I'm not going to leave Cassidy. I've just figured out how to get her back into my life. The board is going to have to accept some kind of compromise. I suggest you and I go in there united."

"What do you have in mind?" Sam asked.

"A joint venture. Granddaddy knew you and I were the future, and I'm not sure that he didn't mean for us to somehow work out an agreement."

Sam laughed. "He didn't. He set us against each other because we both respond to a challenge."

"True. So can you do it?"

"If you can convince the board? Then, yes, I'll go for it."

"If the board doesn't meet my terms, I'm walking. I've given this company everything, and to have them tell me who I can marry is going too far."

Donovan had thought about it good and hard before he'd come to the office today. Leaving Cassidy behind in bed had been difficult. He'd wanted to be there when she woke so he could make sure she understood that he wasn't letting her walk out of his life.

"They won't respond to a threat," Sam said.

"They will respond to the bottom line. You and I have already impacted revenues in ways that Theo never could and won't be able to. He's too stuck in the old way of doing business."

"Right. Do you have documentation to back up the figures?"

"I do," Donovan said. He took out his Black-Berry and sent a quick text to Marcus. Then he sent another note to Cassidy. Just a quick one to tell her that he needed to see her as soon as he was done with this meeting.

Because if this morning had done one thing, it had reinforced to him how much he loved her—and he needed to tell her that.

"We're ready for you both now," Theo said from the doorway.

"I need a word with Donovan." His mother stood behind his uncle.

"Fine. We can wait five minutes," Theo said.

His mother began walking down the hall toward his office. "Mom?"

She turned. "We can't talk in the hallway."

He nodded and followed her past Karin, his assistant, who glanced up, arching her eyebrows at him. He signaled her to hold his calls.

His mother walked over to the window overlooking downtown Charleston and crossed her arms.

"What is it?" he asked.

"I owe you and Cassidy an apology."

Okay. *That* he hadn't expected. "Why?"

"For hiding your marriage from the board and Sam. I know that you meant to hide it from the public just temporarily until Van was born, but I kept hoping that the marriage would fall apart."

"It isn't going to," Donovan said. "Her family isn't as bad as you make them out to be."

"I know. That's why I'm apologizing. I told the board that you two are married and that the marriage is a solid match."

"Did that sway them?" he asked, aware that his mother had in her own way gone to bat for him. And he appreciated it more than he'd thought he would.

She shrugged. "It was a written vote, not vocal, so I have no idea of the outcome."

"Thanks, Mom. What changed your mind about Cassidy and the Franzones?"

"Cassidy did. She brought Van by to visit us yesterday. She was very frank with your father and I about the lies you'd told her and how that made her feel. She said she had no idea how much longer your marriage would last, but she wanted Van to know his grandparents."

Donovan wasn't surprised. Cassidy was kinder than he deserved. And if she had any idea of the things his mother had done, apparently that hadn't stopped Cassidy from doing the right thing.

"That girl is a keeper, Donovan," his mother said.

He agreed with his mother, which didn't happen that often.

As his mother left and he prepared to go to the boardroom, his BlackBerry vibrated. He glanced at the screen to see a message from Cassidy, informing him that she was aware that he had to divorce her to become CEO. He stared at the words, wondering how she knew what had happened in the boardroom.

He dialed her number and got her voice mail. He left a message, but had the feeling that Cassidy wasn't interested in listening to anything he had to say.

Cassidy and Van were having a quiet evening at home. Well, at her home. She hadn't been able to go back to the mansion she shared with Donovan. She also wanted to be away from her family, as they were acting as though they had a right to make decisions in her life. She'd set them straight and told Adam to mind his own business.

The doorbell rang just before seven and she opened the door to find Jimmy standing there.

"What are you doing here?"

"Delivery again."

"I don't need any soup."

"It's not soup."

He handed her a padded envelope and gave her a

smile before he walked back to his car. She closed the door and stared bemusedly at the envelope in her hand. It had her name written on it in very distinctive handwriting—Donovan's.

She wasn't ready to deal with anything else from him right now. The jewelry box sat on the table in the foyer, still unopened. She tossed the envelope next to it and walked back to the family room, where Van was sleeping in his playpen.

Ten minutes later her cell phone rang and she checked the caller ID before answering it. "Hey, Emma."

"Hey, girl. Did you open the envelope?"

"Which one?"

"The one Jimmy delivered."

"No, and how do you know about it?"

"Because I'm coming over to babysit."

"I don't want to talk to Donovan."

"Trust me, on this you're going to want to at least give him a chance to explain."

"I've already given him three chances with my heart, and each time he's let me down."

"I know. If you didn't love him then I'd say to ignore him, but you do, so give him a chance to explain and make things up to you."

"What does he have planned?"

"I don't know. Open the envelope. I'm going to be there in fifteen minutes."

Cassidy hung up and went back to the foyer. She brought the envelope and jewelry box into the living room and sat down where she could see Van.

She opened the envelope first and inside found an invitation requesting her presence at the yacht club tonight at nine.

She shook her head. Romance and romantic gestures weren't going to win her over. But a part of her…okay, all of her, wanted her relationship with Donovan to work. As hurt as she was by his actions, she still hadn't had time to fall out of love with him. She didn't know if she'd ever be able to.

She opened the jewelry box and found inside a platinum charm bracelet. There was only one charm on it. A photo of her, Van and Donovan, a small version of the photo that hung by Van's crib at her parents' house. On the back of the charm was a small engraving that read, This is my world.

She felt a sting of tears as she read it. She wasn't sure what Donovan had in mind for later this evening, but she knew now she was going to go and hear him out. She owed it to the both of them to give their relationship one last chance.

She took the baby monitor down the hall to her bedroom and got changed out of her jeans and shirt into a cocktail-length sundress. She put her makeup on with a steady hand and touched up her curls.

When Emma arrived a few minutes later, she was

almost ready to go. She put on her wedding rings and her charm bracelet.

"I'm going to take Van to my place for the night," Emma said.

"Emma…"

"If you need to come and get him before morning, don't worry. But I have the feeling you're going to be otherwise occupied."

She bit her lower lip. She needed more than another sexy night in Donovan's arms. But she had no idea if he could give her anything more. Romance was fine, but she needed his heart. She really needed him to be the man she'd always believed him to be.

A limo arrived just after Emma, and she hugged her friend and dropped a kiss on Van's head as she left.

In the backseat of the limo she found another envelope. She opened it, and a piece of vellum paper dropped out. On the paper was a poem written by Christopher Brennan called "Because She Would Ask Me Why I Loved Her."

The poem was beautiful and sweet, and the scrawled *I love you* at the bottom made her heart beat a little faster. She wanted to believe that Donovan was making this gesture because he loved her, but a part of her—the part jaded by his betrayals—feared he was going to ask her to remain his secret wife.

Twelve

Donovan was waiting on the dock when the limo pulled up. He had spent the evening making sure every detail was in place. For once, he was nervous, but not because he was afraid of the outcome. He'd always been a winner, and there was no way he'd settle for anything less than complete victory with Cassidy tonight.

"Good evening, Cassidy," he said as he took her hand and helped her out of the back of the car.

"Donovan."

The night sky was filled with stars and a warm tropical breeze stirred off the water. "Thank you for joining me."

"You're welcome. I'll admit I came only because I want to hear what you have to say."

"Did you read my notes?"

"I did."

"And?"

She hesitated.

"I love you, Cassidy."

"Did you lose your job today?" she asked.

Not exactly the response he'd been looking for.

"What does that have to do with anything?"

"Adam said—"

"Adam doesn't know everything."

"No, but I thought Sam did."

Donovan shook his head. "Let's go onto my yacht. I'll tell you all about the day if you want."

She followed him onto the yacht. His chef had prepared some hors d'oeuvres and they were set out near the stern.

"My uncle and the board gave me an ultimatum, which you obviously heard about—leave you, or forfeit the chairmanship. I declined their offer and countered with a joint chairmanship.

"Sam and I have really made a difference in the company bottom line, and we decided we both should be at the helm."

"And they didn't go for it," she said.

"Why are you so sure that they said no?"

"Why else would you be trying so hard to hold on

to me unless you lost the company? That was your number one priority."

He shook his head, regretting the fact that he'd let her down and made her feel as if she didn't mean as much to him as his job did. He'd wanted his grandfather's respect, had craved a chance to make his mark in the world, but over the short course of his marriage, he had realized that being a husband and father was the one thing that mattered most.

"They took our offer. Sam and I are co-CEOs. I'm telling you how I feel about you because, when I thought I was going to lose everything, I didn't feel devastated."

"You didn't?" she asked.

He shook his head and drew her into his arms. "Instead, I thought about you and Van and the family we were starting, and I looked at my relatives who sit on the board. Even though they also represent the investors in the company, I knew that family was the most important thing.

"That *you* were the most important thing in my life," he said, leaning down to kiss her. "You and Van.

"I love you, Cassidy Franzone Tolley. And I want to marry you again in front of the world so that everyone knows you are mine."

Cassidy was crying, but she was also smiling— the brightest smile he'd ever seen. "I love you, too, Donovan."

"Will you marry me again?"

"No," she said, and his heart nearly stopped. "I don't need a ceremony in front of the world."

He let out a breath, overwhelmed by his love for this woman. "What do you need?"

"You," she said.

* * * * *

The Colton family is back!
Enjoy a sneak preview of
COLTON'S SECRET SERVICE
by Marie Ferrarella,
part of
THE COLTONS: FAMILY FIRST *miniseries.*

Available from Silhouette Romantic Suspense
in September 2008.

He cautioned himself to be leery. He was human and he'd been conned before. But never by anyone nearly so attractive. Never by anyone he'd felt so attracted to.

In her defense, Nick supposed that Georgie could actually be telling him the truth. That she was a victim in all this. He had his people back in California checking her out, to make sure she was who she said she was and had, as she claimed, not even been near a computer but on the road these last few months that the threats had been made.

In the meantime, he was doing his own checking out. Up close and exceedingly personal. So personal he could feel his blood stirring.

It had been a long time since he'd thought of himself as anything other than a law enforcement agent of one type or other. But Georgeann Grady made him remember that beneath the oaths he had taken and his devotion to duty, there beat the heart of a man.

A man who'd been far too long without the touch of a woman.

He watched as the light from the fireplace caressed the outline of Georgie's small, trim, jean-clad body as she moved about the rustic living room that could have easily come off the set of a Hollywood Western. Except that it was genuine.

As genuine as she claimed to be?

Something inside of him hoped so.

He wasn't supposed to be taking sides. His only interest in being here was to guarantee Senator Joe Colton's safety as the latter continued to make his bid for the presidency. Everything else was supposed to be secondary, but, Nick had to silently admit, that was just a wee bit hard to remember right now.

Earlier, before she'd put her precocious handful of a daughter to bed, Georgie had fed his appetite by whipping up some kind of a delicious concoction out of the vegetables she'd pulled from her garden. Vegetables that, by all rights, should have been withered and dried. She'd mentioned that a friend came by on occasion to weed and tend it. Still, it surprised him that somehow she'd managed to make something mouthwatering out of it.

Almost as mouthwatering as she looked to him right at this moment.

Again, he was reminded of the appetite that hadn't been fed, hadn't been satisfied.

And wasn't going to be, Nick sternly told himself. At least not now. Maybe later, when things took on a more definite shape and all the questions in his head were answered to his satisfaction, there would be time to explore this feeling. This woman. But not now.

Damn it.

"Sorry about the lack of light," Georgie said, breaking into his train of thought as she turned around to face him. If she noticed the way he was looking at her, she gave no indication. "But I don't see a point in paying for electricity if I'm not going to be here. Besides, Emmie really enjoys camping out. She likes roughing it."

"And you?" Nick asked, moving closer to her, so close that a whisper would have trouble fitting in. "What do you like?"

The very breath stopped in Georgie's throat as she looked up at him.

"I think you've got a fair shot of guessing that one," she told him softly.

* * * * *

Silhouette®

Romantic
SUSPENSE

Sparked by Danger,
Fueled by Passion.

The Coltons Are Back!
Marie Ferrarella
Colton's Secret Service

The Coltons: Family First

On a mission to protect a senator, Secret Service agent
Nick Sheffield tracks down a threatening message only
to discover Georgie Gradie Colton, a rodeo-riding single
mom, who insists on her innocence. Nick is instantly
taken with the feisty redhead, but vows not to let his
feelings interfere with his mission. Now he must figure
out if this woman is conning him or if he can trust her
and the passion they share....

Available September wherever books are sold.

Look for upcoming Colton titles
from Silhouette Romantic Suspense:

RANCHER'S REDEMPTION by Beth Cornelison, Available October
THE SHERIFF'S AMNESIAC BRIDE by Linda Conrad, Available November
SOLDIER'S SECRET CHILD by Caridad Piñeiro, Available December
BABY'S WATCH by Justine Davis, Available January 2009
A HERO OF HER OWN by Carla Cassidy, Available February 2009

Visit Silhouette Books at www.eHarlequin.com   SRS27598

REQUEST YOUR FREE BOOKS!

2 FREE NOVELS
PLUS 2
FREE GIFTS!

Passionate, Powerful, Provocative!

YES! Please send me 2 FREE Silhouette Desire® novels and my 2 FREE gifts (gifts are worth about $10). After receiving them, if I don't wish to receive any more books, I can return the shipping statement marked "cancel". If I don't cancel, I will receive 6 brand-new novels every month and be billed just $4.05 per book in the U.S. or $4.74 per book in Canada, plus 25¢ shipping and handling per book and applicable taxes, if any*. That's a savings of almost 15% off the cover price! I understand that accepting the 2 free books and gifts places me under no obligation to buy anything. I can always return a shipment and cancel at any time. Even if I never buy another book, the two free books and gifts are mine to keep forever.   225 SDN ERVX 326 SDN ERVM

Name	(PLEASE PRINT)	
Address		Apt. #
City	State/Prov.	Zip/Postal Code

Signature (if under 18, a parent or guardian must sign)

Mail to the **Silhouette Reader Service:**
IN U.S.A.: P.O. Box 1867, Buffalo, NY 14240-1867
IN CANADA: P.O. Box 609, Fort Erie, Ontario L2A 5X3

Not valid to current subscribers of Silhouette Desire books.

Want to try two free books from another line?
Call 1-800-873-8635 or visit www.morefreebooks.com.

* Terms and prices subject to change without notice. N.Y. residents add applicable sales tax. Canadian residents will be charged applicable provincial taxes and GST. Offer not valid in Quebec. This offer is limited to one order per household. All orders subject to approval. Credit or debit balances in a customer's account(s) may be offset by any other outstanding balance owed by or to the customer. Please allow 4 to 6 weeks for delivery. Offer available while quantities last.

Your Privacy: Silhouette Books is committed to protecting your privacy. Our Privacy Policy is available online at www.eHarlequin.com or upon request from the Reader Service. From time to time we make our lists of customers available to reputable third parties who may have a product or service of interest to you. If you would prefer we not share your name and address, please check here. ☐

SDES08R

COMING NEXT MONTH